BLUE-EYED DEVIL

BLUE-EYED DEVIL

ROBERT B. PARKER

LARGE PRINT PRESS
A part of Gale, Cengage Learning

GALE
CENGAGE Learning™

Detroit • New York • San Francisco • New Haven, Conn • Waterville, Maine • London

GALE
CENGAGE Learning·

The text of this Large Print edition is unabridged.
Other aspects of the book may vary from the original edition.
Set in 16 pt. Plantin.

LIBRARY OF CONGRESS CATALOGING-IN-PUBLICATION DATA

Parker, Robert B., 1932–2010.
  Blue-eyed devil / by Emily Brightwell.
  p. cm.
  ISBN-13: 978-1-4104-2450-1
  ISBN-10: 1-4104-2450-2
  1. Cole, Virgil (Fictitious character)—Fiction. 2. Hitch, Everett (Fictitious character)—Fiction. 3. Large type books. I. Title.
  PS3566.A686B57 2010b
  813'.54—dc22   2010009599

ISBN 13: 978-1-59413-456-2 (pbk. : alk. paper)
ISBN 10: 1-59413-456-1 (pbk. : alk. paper)

Published in 2011 by arrangement with G. P. Putnam's Sons, a member of Penguin Group (USA) Inc.

Printed in the United States of America
  1 2 3 4 5   15 14 13 12 11
ED098

*For Joan: blue-eyed and devilish,
in exactly the right proportion*

1

Law enforcement in Appaloosa had once been Virgil Cole and me. Now there were a chief of police and twelve policemen. Our third day back in town, the chief invited us to the office for a talk.

He was tall and very fat in a derby hat and a dark suit, with a star on his vest, and big black-handled Colt in a Huckleberry inside his coat. Standing silently around the room were four of his police officers, dressed in white shirts and dark pants, each with a Colt on his hip.

The chief gestured for us to sit. Virgil sat. I leaned my shotgun on the wall by the door and sat beside him.

"Heard 'bout both of you," he said. "Heard 'bout that thing, too. What's it fire, grapeshot?"

"It's an eight-gauge," I said. "Good for grouse."

"Or fucking hippopotamuses," the chief said.

"Them, too," I said.

"Name's Amos Callico," he said. "Thought we should have a chitchat."

Virgil nodded.

"You're Virgil Cole," Callico said.

"I am," Virgil said. "Big fella here with the eight-gauge is Everett Hitch."

"I know who he is," Callico said.

Virgil nodded again.

"What I hear 'bout you is mostly good," Callico said.

Virgil looked at me.

"Mostly," he said.

"Probably meant 'all,' " I said.

Callico paid no attention. He took a cigar from a box on his desk, didn't offer us one, trimmed it and lit it, and got it burning right. The four policemen stood silently, watching us.

"I know your reputation, Cole," he said. "And I know that you ran the town, 'fore I got here. And I want you both to understand that you don't run it now."

"That would be you," Virgil said.

"And I've got a dozen officers to back me," Callico said.

Virgil didn't say anything.

"On the other hand, none of them are like

you," Callico said. "I could use couple of gun hands like you."

Virgil shook his head slowly.

"Pay you fifty a month," Callico said.

"Nope," Virgil said.

"Make you a sergeant," Callico said.

"Nope."

"You speakin' for Hitch, too?" Callico said.

"Yep."

"Why the hell not?" Callico said.

Virgil looked at me.

"You think you're important," I said to Callico. "Virgil don't think anybody's important. Bad match."

Virgil nodded.

"That right, Cole?" Callico said.

" 'Tis," Virgil said.

Callico puffed on his cigar and blew some smoke past the lit end. He studied it for a moment.

"So, what are you going to do in town?" Callico said.

"Sit on my porch," Virgil said. "Drink a little whiskey. Play some cards."

"That's all?" Callico said.

"See what develops," Virgil said.

Callico smoked his cigar some more. Then he looked at me.

"You boys done a nice job when you was

9

in this office," Callico said. "Bragg and the Shelton brothers and all."

Virgil nodded. Callico looked at me.

"Heard you killed Randall Bragg 'fore you left town," Callico said.

"I did," I said.

"Why?"

"Self-defense," I said.

"Heard it was over a woman," Callico said.

"I got nothing to do," I said, "with what you hear."

"Was it over a woman?"

I shook my head.

"You know why he killed Bragg?" Callico said to Virgil.

"Bragg come at him with a gun," Virgil said.

"Why?"

"Have to ask Bragg," Virgil said.

"Bragg's dead," Callico said.

"So he is," Virgil said.

We all sat and thought about that. Callico nodded slowly.

"Don't want no trouble from you boys," he said.

"Don't plan to give you none," Virgil said.

Callico looked at me.

"Me, either," I said.

"I'll hold you to that," Callico said.

Virgil stood.

"Nice meeting you," he said.

He looked around the room at the four policemen.

"And you fellas," Virgil said.

He turned and left, and I followed him.

On the street, I said to Virgil, "We're gonna have trouble with him."

"I believe we are," Virgil said.

2

Virgil's house hadn't changed much in the time we'd been away. Allie and Laurel cleaned it up as soon as we arrived back in Appaloosa, and we moved right in. I bunked with Virgil in one bedroom, and Allie slept with Laurel in the second.

All four of us were sitting on the front porch sipping whiskey in the early evening while it was still light, when a tall, thin man with a big mustache walked up the front path. It was Stringer, the chief sheriff's deputy.

"Ev'nin," he said.

"Stringer," Virgil said.

"I'm down to pick up a prisoner, heard you folks was back in town. Thought you might be drinking whiskey."

"Sit," I said. "Have some."

Stringer adjusted his gun belt a little and sat.

"Allie," Virgil said. "You remember

Deputy Stringer."

"I don't recall us meeting," Allie said.

"You was with the Shelton brothers," Virgil said. "Probably thinking 'bout other things."

Allie nodded.

"At the train," she said.

"That's me," Stringer said.

"How do you do," she said to Stringer, and made a small curtsy.

"Glad you're well," Stringer said. "Who's this young lady?"

"Her name's Laurel," Virgil said. "She don't say much. Laurel, this here is Deputy Stringer."

Laurel looked at Stringer and nodded slowly and made her small curtsy. Then she went to Virgil and whispered to him. He whispered back. She whispered again.

"Well, sure, sort of like Pony Flores," Virgil said.

"She shy?" Stringer said.

"Indian took her," Virgil said. "She had a pretty bad time till we got her back."

"Her folks are dead," Allie said. "I'm looking out for her."

"Since we got her back," I said, "won't talk to nobody 'cept Virgil."

Stringer sipped some whiskey.

"Who's Pony Flores?" Stringer said.

13

"Tracker," Virgil said. "Helped us get her back."

Laurel whispered again to Virgil. He listened and nodded.

"He gave her a gun," Virgil said. "She wants to show it to you."

Stringer nodded. Laurel took the derringer out of the pocket of her pinafore and held it out in the palm of her hand. Stringer looked at it carefully.

"That's a very fine derringer," he said.

He looked at Virgil.

"Loaded," he said.

"She knows how to use it," Virgil said. "Makes her feel safer."

Stringer nodded.

"What are you boys gonna do here?" Stringer said.

"We're posturing that," Virgil said.

"Or pondering," I said.

"Pondering," Virgil said. "That's what we're doing. Everett went to the Military Academy."

"Could speak to the sheriff for you," Stringer said.

"Foraged up some money in Brimstone," Virgil said. "We figure to take some time and look around."

"You boys good at anything but gun work?" Stringer said.

"Might be," Virgil said.

"Like what?" Stringer said.

"We're ponderin' that, too," Virgil said.

"Meet the new chief of police?" Stringer said.

His voice was neutral, but there was something in the way he said "chief of police."

"Yep," Virgil said.

"And?" Stringer said.

"Offered us a job," Virgil said.

"Which you turned down," Stringer said.

"Everett and me don't like him," Virgil said.

Stringer studied the surface of his whiskey for a moment and then drank some.

"How come?" Stringer said.

Virgil looked at me.

"He annoyed Virgil," I said. "Kinda full of himself."

Stringer nodded.

"Don't make no mistake with him," Stringer said. "He's a horse's ass, okay, but he knows what he wants. He'll do what he needs to get it. He can shoot, and he will. Got some people working for him can shoot."

"Twelve people working for him," I said.

"Town got big fast," Stringer said.

"Virgil and me ran it with two," I said. "It

get six times bigger?"

"More people work for you, more power you got," Stringer said. "Callico's ambitious."

"He want to be sheriff?" I said.

"It's the next step," Stringer said.

"To what?" Virgil said.

"Governor."

"Why's he want to be governor," Virgil said.

"Probably 'cause it's the next step to senator," Stringer said. "I don't know what Callico wants."

"What kind of lawman is he?" Virgil said.

"Tough, strict, fair enough, I think," Stringer said. "But he got no heart."

"Heart don't do you much good," Virgil said.

Stringer smiled.

" 'Course it doesn't," he said. "Makes you soft."

"Get you killed," Virgil said.

Stringer said, "You think Virgil Cole got heart, Laurel."

Laurel was sitting next to Virgil with Allie on her other side. She showed no sign of having heard Stringer's question.

"She hear me?" Stringer said.

"She don't much talk with anybody but Virgil," I said.

"Hell," Stringer said.

Laurel leaned in close to Virgil and whispered to him. Virgil smiled. He looked at me for a moment, then at Stringer.

"Laurel claims I got the most heart in the world," he said.

3

The Boston House had changed hands twice since I had killed Randall Bragg. But Willis McDonough in his starched white shirt was still the head bartender. And he bought us each a drink when Virgil and I went in to say hello.

"New owner's a fella from Chicago named Lamar Speck," Willis said. "Nice enough fella, I guess. You boys looking for work?"

"Might be," Virgil said.

"No peace-officer work, I guess," Willis said.

"I guess," Virgil said.

As always, Virgil was looking at the room, paying no attention, seeing everything. I didn't bother. Virgil would do it anyway, and he saw more than I did.

"Got more peace officers than you can shake a stick at," Willis said.

"Need 'em all?" Virgil said.

Willis shrugged.

"You boys kept things pretty well buttoned up with just two of you."

"So why so many?" I said.

Willis looked around at the near-empty bar, then leaned forward and lowered his voice.

"Might be another plan," he said.

"What?" Virgil said.

"I'm just a bartender," Willis said, "but. . . ."

Virgil waited.

Willis looked around again and leaned in toward us even closer.

"Not much happens around here anymore without Chief Callico having something to do with it," he said softly.

"Payoffs?" Virgil said.

"I'm just the bartender."

"But you hear things," Virgil said.

"I think Mr. Speck gives him money."

"What happens if he don't?" Virgil said.

"There's trouble, police are too busy, ya know? Too busy to get here."

"And you got nobody to keep order?" I said.

Willis shook his head.

"Was a fella named Hector Barnes," Willis said. "Worked the lookout chair with his brother, Chico. But they quit."

"Why?" Virgil said.

Willis shrugged.

"I think the police was bothering them about things."

"They run 'em off?" Virgil said.

Willis shrugged.

"Ain't here no more," he said.

"And Speck is making his payments," Virgil said.

"Might be," Willis said.

"Anybody say anything to the sheriff?" I said.

"He's a day's ride from here," Willis said.

"So?"

"Something might happen to you or your place, by the time the sheriff got to sending a deputy down."

"So, how come you're telling us," I said.

"Figured it might be a job opening for you boys," Willis said.

"Keepin' the peace in the Boston House?" I said.

"I tole Mr. Speck I'd speak to you, first time you come in," Willis said.

"Should we talk to Mr. Speck," I said.

"I can arrange it," Willis said.

I looked at Virgil. He nodded slowly. I nodded with him.

"Why don't you," Virgil said to Willis.

4

Lamar Speck was a little skinny guy with a big Adam's apple and a prominent nose. He dressed like a dandy. Black coat with velvet lapels, a red-and-gold vest, striped trousers. He sat at a big rolltop desk in the back office of the saloon, and swiveled around in his chair and stood when Willis showed us in.

"Mr. Cole," he said. "Mr. Hitch. A pleasure."

We agreed that it was a pleasure.

"I understand that you gentlemen are looking for work," Speck said.

"Might be," Virgil said.

"Sit," Speck said. "Please."

We sat. McDonough was looking at Virgil as he talked. Everybody always talked to Virgil.

"I have of course heard of you gentlemen, especially, Mr. Cole. And of course I know you used to be the lawmen in town."

"We were," Virgil said.

"And I know that most of our citizens respect you both," Speck said.

"They surely do," Virgil said.

He didn't show it. But I knew Virgil was getting restless. It drove him crazy when people rambled on, except when it was him.

"So, I thought to myself, *Lamar, here's a chance to get some first-rate help.* If you boys will agree, I'll hire you, and if there's trouble, you'll take care of it."

"How much?" Virgil said.

Speck told him.

"You don't have anybody sitting lookout?" Virgil said.

"The police arrested my last one," Speck said. "Turns out he was wanted in Kansas."

"Kansas," Virgil said, and looked at me.

"The police keep a sharp eye in Appaloosa," I said.

"We run our own show," Virgil said. "Post a list of rules, people obey them or they leave. People give us trouble, we shoot them."

"Shoot?"

"You think people gonna obey the rules 'cause they like us?" Virgil said.

"Well, ah, no, of course not, I guess."

"They obey the rules 'cause they know we'll shoot," Virgil says. "Which means maybe, now and then, we'll have to."

"Well, I . . . certainly. You know this work best."

"Police gonna be helpful?" I said.

"I'm sure they will be pleased to have help," Speck said.

"They been helpful in the past?" I said.

"They are often very busy," Speck said.

"Ain't had any trouble with Callico?" Virgil said.

"Certainly not," Speck said. "Except for my lookout."

Virgil nodded.

"We'll come by in the morning," Virgil said. "Give a list of our rules. You agree to post them. We'll start work."

Speck stood and put out his hand. Virgil ignored it.

"Virgil don't shake hands," I said. "Nothing personal."

"Oh," Speck said. "Oh, well, very good. I'll look forward to seeing you tomorrow."

As we stood on the porch outside the Boston House, Virgil said, "You ain't wanted in Kansas, are you?"

"No," I said. "You?"

"Nope."

"Maybe Callico's just enforcing the law," I said.

"That's getting to seem harder than it used to," Virgil said.

5

The pay was regular at the Boston House, and the work was easy. Most people in Appaloosa had heard of Virgil Cole.

When things were slow, Virgil and I would drink coffee with the whores in the back of the room, or lean on the bar and talk with the bartenders. When the place was busy we'd move through the room, making sure nobody was heeled and, occasionally, soothing a belligerent.

I was up front one evening, talking with Willis, when one of the whores yelled for Virgil. I looked. A man in a fancy frock coat had hold of the whore's arm and was trying to drag her out of her chair. Virgil walked over. I picked up my eight-gauge and strolled up to where I could watch Virgil's back.

The whore's name was Emma Scarlet. She was a pleasant whore, and I liked her.

"I'm not going with you," she said.

"You're selling your ass," he said, "and my money's as good as anybody's."

"You don't like to fuck," Emma said to the man in the frock coat. "You like to hurt people."

"You can let her arm be," Virgil said to the man in the frock coat.

"Who the fuck are you?" the man said.

He was tall and slim with long, blond hair and a white shirt buttoned to the neck. I didn't see a gun.

"Virgil Cole," Virgil said.

"What makes this your business," the man said.

"I'm not going to fuck with this," Virgil said. "You let her go, or I'll kill you."

The man let go of the whore's arm and took a step back, as if Virgil had pushed him.

"Kill me?"

"That's better," Virgil said.

"Kill me?" the man said. "Over a fucking whore in a saloon?"

"Got trouble with this whore, find another one," Virgil said.

"Some other place," Emma said. "Nobody here's gonna let him do anything."

Virgil nodded.

"Any of you ladies care to do business with this gentleman?" Virgil said.

No one said anything. Several of the

whores shook their heads.

"Guess not," Virgil said to the man. "Try down the street."

"You're kicking me out?" the man said. "Because the whores don't like me?"

"I am," Virgil said, and stepped aside to let him pass.

"You got no idea who I am, do you?"

"I don't," Virgil said, and nodded toward the door.

"My name's Nicholas Laird," he said. "That mean anything to you?"

"Means none of these ladies want your business," Virgil said.

He took hold of Laird's right arm with his left hand. Laird tried to shake it off and couldn't.

"We'll walk to the door," Virgil said.

"You're heeled," Laird said. "And I'm not. And you got the shotgun over there."

"Bad odds," Virgil said.

"Next time you see me," Laird said, "odds are gonna be different."

Virgil's face changed slightly. No one else probably could tell. But I knew he was smiling.

"Maybe not," Virgil said.

6

We were drinking coffee at the bar with Willis McDonough.

"Would you really have shot him?" Willis asked.

"Certain," Virgil said.

"She's a whore," Willis said.

"She is," Virgil said. "But she ain't a slave."

Willis nodded and looked like he didn't get it, but he didn't need to.

"Well, you bit a pretty big end off the plug," Willis said. "His old man is General Horatio Laird. Took over Bragg's place after" — Willis looked at me — "after he, ah, died. Bought that Scots bull, too."

"Black angus," I said.

"Yeah," Willis said. "Them, and the cows, and made a killing with 'em. People back east was eatin' them fast as Laird could slaughter the steers."

"Rich man?" I said.

"Damn straight," Willis said.

"What's the 'general' for."

"Confederate army."

"Still hanging on to it," I said.

"Proud of it," Willis said. "Proud of a lot of things. But the kid ain't one of them."

"Nicholas," Virgil said.

"The general must have done some bad stuff in his life, 'cause Nicholas is a big punishment," Willis said.

Virgil didn't seem to be listening. He scanned the room aimlessly. But I knew he heard everything. Just like he saw everything.

"Wild?" I said.

"Thinks he's a gun hand," Willis said. "Tell me he practices an hour every day with a Colt."

"Ever shoot at live targets?" Virgil said.

"Heard he might," Willis said. " 'Specially he got some folks behind him."

"Folks," Virgil said.

"General's getting on," Willis said. "He's tryin' to let the kid run things, so he'll be ready when the general steps off the train. Kid has hired himself some second-rate riffraff up there worse than Bragg had."

"Be some bad riffraff," Virgil said. "They shooters?"

"Most of 'em couldn't hit a bull in the ass

with a shovel," Willis said.

"Useless, too," Virgil said.

7

It was a dark gray day, when Amos Callico came into the saloon, with four of his policemen. The four policemen all carried Winchesters.

"Like to sit with you boys for a minute," Callico said.

We sat at a table up front near the bar. The four policemen ranged along the walls near us. The tables around us were empty. One of the bartenders brought a bottle and three glasses.

"Understand you hired on here," Callico said.

He poured himself some whiskey and offered the bottle toward us. Virgil and I declined.

"That right?" Callico said.

"It is," Virgil said.

"Bouncers," Callico said.

"Correct," Virgil said.

"Got you a big list of rules," Callico said,

and nodded without looking at the rules posted on the wall.

"We do," Virgil said.

"Pretty much same rules you had for the town when you was marshal," Callico said.

"Pretty much," Virgil said.

"Just want to be sure you remember that you ain't marshal now," Callico said.

"I remember," Virgil said.

Callico looked at me for the first time.

"You?" he said.

"I remember, too," I said.

He looked at the eight-gauge leaning against the edge of the table.

"You haul that fucking blunderbuss around with you everywhere?" he said.

"I do," I said.

"For God's sake, why?" Callico said.

"Same reason you have your boys carry Winchesters in a saloon," I said. "Folks get the idea you're serious."

Callico looked at me without expression for a moment. Then he turned back to Virgil.

"Why do you suppose Speck hired you?" Callico said.

"Keep order," Virgil said.

"I'm the one keeps order in Appaloosa," Callico said.

"Well, that's by-God comforting," Virgil

said. "We run into trouble we'll be sure to holler for you."

"You should have hollered for me already," Callico said.

Virgil looked at me.

"You know any reason we should have hollered for the police?" Virgil said.

"Nope."

"You threw Nicky Laird out of here, couple days ago, for a damn whore."

"Several damn whores," Virgil said.

"He's a highly regarded citizen of this town, and his father is a close personal friend of mine."

"Nice," Virgil said.

"You embarrassed him in public," Callico said.

"Man embarrassed himself," Virgil said.

"Boys," Callico said, and poured himself more whiskey. "This is exactly why I don't want no vigilante law enforcing going on. There's a distinguished citizen being insulted by some whores and you side with the whores."

He stopped, drank some of his whiskey, and shook his head slowly.

"You boys know the county sheriff's chief deputy," Callico said.

"Stringer," Virgil said.

Callico nodded.

"He was in town picking up a prisoner. Got a lot of regard for you boys."

"Stringer's a good man," Virgil said.

"And I got a high regard for you both. I know your reputation," Callico said. "But you can't run a town with two different sets of law."

"Welcome to borrow ours," Virgil said.

Callico slammed his hand loudly on the table. Virgil didn't appear to notice.

"Goddamn it," he said. "I don't want either one of you working here. That put it plain enough?"

"I'd say it was," he answered. "You say so, Everett?"

"I do," I said.

"Then you'll quit," Callico said.

"No," Virgil said.

"No?" Callico said. "I won't take no."

"Everett," Virgil said, "I think Chief Callico is trying to intimate us. . . ."

Virgil paused and frowned and shook his head.

"No," he said. "That ain't right. What am I trying to say, Everett?"

"Intimidate?" I said.

"That's it," Virgil said. "I think the chief is trying to intimidate us."

As quietly as I could, I cocked both hammers on the eight-gauge.

"Goddamn it, I'm telling you plain what I want," Callico said.

"Amos," Virgil said. "Me 'n Everett don't much care what you want."

"You defying me?" Callico said.

"By God," Virgil said. "I believe we are."

"There's five armed men here," Callico said.

Virgil said nothing.

"You're willing to die rather than let me run you off?" Callico said.

Virgil shook his head.

"Don't expect to die," he said.

"Against five men?" Callico said.

"Expect me and Everett can kill you all," Virgil said.

Everyone was still, except Callico. I could hear him breathing in and out, his chest heaving slowly. Then he, too, quieted. Very slowly he put both hands flat on the table-top.

"Don't get ahead shooting people up in a saloon," he said, and looked at us.

Then he stood and jerked his head at the officers along the wall.

"We'll talk again," he said to Virgil.

And they filed out.

"Be my guess it ain't over," I said.

"When he finds an excuse," Virgil said.

8

If we stayed around the house in the morning until Allie got up, she set right in cooking us breakfast. So we tried to get out, before she woke up, and went to eat at Café Paris. Since I wasn't a lawman these days, and I didn't expect to shoot anybody, I left the eight-gauge in the house.

"We got to eat supper with her sometimes, so's not to hurt her feelin's," Virgil said. "But I can't face her cooking in the morning."

"How's the rest of it going," I said.

"She don't seem so crazy," Virgil said.

"Maybe 'cause she got Laurel to take care of," I said.

"Maybe," Virgil said.

"Makes her feel important," I said.

"She's important to me," Virgil said.

"I know," I said.

"Sex life be better, though," Virgil said, "Allie wasn't sleepin' with Laurel."

"Maybe I could arrange for Laurel and me to take long walks in the evening," I said.

"Might help," Virgil said.

"And," I said, "soon as we settle in, I'll get a place of my own."

"I know," Virgil said. "But I ain't sure Laurel can sleep by herself."

"No," I said. "Probably can't."

Virgil paid for breakfast.

"So we're back to the long walks," I said.

We stood.

"Thing is," Virgil said as we left Café Paris, "Allie says she feels funny doing it now that there's a child in the house."

"Even if the child is out for walk?" I said. "With me?"

Virgil shrugged. We strolled along Main Street to the Boston House and sat on the front porch and looked at the town.

"Be worth a try," Virgil said.

We sat without talking. There was nothing uncomfortable in the silence. We could sit quiet for a long time. And we'd shared a lot of silences in the years we'd been together.

The land north of Appaloosa rose gradually through the mesquite. A wagon road ran up the rise to the edge of town, where it became Main Street. From town, unless you were at the very northern edge, you couldn't see the road. It was as if Appaloosa stood

37

long at the edge of a cliff, and when anything entered town from that direction it seemed simply to appear. There wasn't a lot of traffic yet on Main Street. Two freight wagons appeared, each hauled by four big draft horses, their wide hooves kicking up little scatters of dust as they came. The early stage to Blue Rock went past us, heading north with two passengers and the driver up top next to the shotgun messenger.

"Town don't bustle much," Virgil said, "this early."

"Later," I said. "It'll bustle later."

Virgil nodded toward the north end of Main Street.

"Couple riders," he said.

I looked.

"So?" I said.

"Recognize anybody?" Virgil said.

"Not yet," I said.

"One on the left'll be Pony Flores," Virgil said.

I studied the riders.

Then I said, "I believe it will."

9

The riders pulled up and sat their horses in front of the Boston House.

"Pony," Virgil said.

Pony nodded at him. His Stetson was tipped forward, shading his face.

"Thought you was going to live Chiricahua for a spell," I said.

Pony shrugged and tipped his head toward the rider beside him.

"My brother," he said, "Kha-to-nay."

We said, "Hello."

Kha-to-nay had no reaction.

"He speak English?" Virgil said.

"Can," Pony said. "Won't."

"Don't like English?" Virgil said.

"He raised Chiricahua," Pony said. "Don't like white men."

"He understand what we say?" I asked.

"Sure," Pony said. "But only listen Chiricahua. Only talk Chiricahua."

"Should introduce him to Laurel," I said.

"She only talks Virgil."

"Chiquita," Pony said. "She is well?"

"Doin' fine," Virgil said. "Kinda quiet, is all."

Kha-to-nay was motionless on his horse. As far as I could tell, watching him sit a horse, he was a little shorter than Pony, and a little wider. Pony had on buckskin leggings and high moccasins. The handle of a knife showed at the top of the right moccasin. He had on a dark blue shirt that might have once belonged to a soldier, and a big horn-handled Colt on a concho-studded belt. There was a Winchester in his saddle scabbard. Kha-to-nay wore a dark suit and a black-and-white striped shirt buttoned up tight to his neck. His black hair came to his shoulders. He, too, had a Winchester, and he wore a bowie knife on his belt.

"You lawmen again?" Pony said.

"Not at present," Virgil said.

Pony nodded.

"Need help," he said.

"Okay," Virgil said.

"How the law in this town?" Pony said.

"Got a police chief," I said. "Name of Amos Callico. Seems pretty set in his ways."

Pony looked at Virgil.

"Don't like him," Virgil said.

40

"You live someplace?" Pony said.

"Got a house," Virgil said.

"We go there and talk," Pony said.

"Sure," Virgil said. "Allie be glad to see you."

We stood, and with Pony and Kha-to-nay walking their horses beside us, we went down Main Street toward Virgil's house.

"What's Kha-to-nay mean, in English?" I said to Pony.

Pony thought a minute.

"Sees a Snake," he said. "I think."

"You think?" I said.

Pony pointed to his head.

"Change into Spanish," he said. "Then Spanish to English."

We could have been speaking Egyptian for all the attention Kha-to-nay paid. He rode silently, his eyes shifting left and right as he rode. We went down to First Street and turned right and walked a block to Front Street, where Virgil's house was.

Allie was on the front porch in a rocker, reading to Laurel. I knew what she was reading. It was a book called *Ladies' Book of Etiquette, Fashion, and Manual of Politeness.* She'd been reading a chapter a day to Laurel since we left Brimstone. I didn't know if it was doing Laurel any good, but Allie appeared to be soaking it up.

41

They both looked up as we came into the small yard. Neither of them said anything for a moment. Then Laurel stood up abruptly and stepped off the porch. She walked to Pony, being careful not to look at Kha-to-nay, and took the derringer out of her apron pocket, and held it out so Pony could see it. Pony smiled, threw a leg over the pommel of his saddle, and slid fluidly off his horse.

"Chiquita," he said.

She jumped into his arms, and he held her, rocking gently side to side. Kha-to-nay sat silent as a stone.

"Pony Flores," Allie said. "How perfectly lovely. Come sit on the porch, you and your friend."

Pony said something to Kha-to-nay in Apache. Kha-to-nay shook his head. Pony spoke again. Kha-to-nay did not answer, nor did he look at any of us.

"My brother is a donkey," Pony said. "But he is my brother."

10

We sat on the porch and passed around a jug of corn whiskey. Allie put a marker in her etiquette book, went to get small glasses for herself and Laurel.

"Ladies don't drink from jugs," Allie said.

Virgil poured a little for each lady, and took a pull from the jug before he handed it to Pony Flores. Laurel sat close beside Virgil and did not look at Kha-to-nay.

Kha-to-nay would not touch the jug or even acknowledge that it existed. But he did finally get off his horse and lean on the porch railing, with his Winchester, looking toward town, standing as far away from the rest of us as possible.

"For true Chiricahua, Blue-Eyed Devil not exist," Pony said. "What Kha-to-nay believe."

"You're a half Mex," Virgil said. "Ain't he?"

"All Chiricahua," Pony said. "Same

43

mother. Different father."

"He hate us all?" I said.

"Like only Chiricahua," Pony said.

"We take away his land?" I said.

"Take away everything," Pony said.

"How you feel about that?"

"You come, take away what Chiricahua have," Pony said. "While ago Chiricahua come and take away from other people. Other people come long time ago, take away." Pony shrugged. "Somebody probably come one day, take away from Blue-Eyed Devil," Pony said. "Happen always."

"S'pose it does," I said. "Kha-to-nay know you feel like that?"

"*Sí,*" Pony said.

"You talk about it?" I said.

"*Sí,*" Pony said. "I think man live now, do what need to be done, keep word, don't think how things be before."

"And Kha-to-nay?" I said.

Pony smiled.

"Say I am only half Chiricahua."

I nodded. Kha-to-nay stared into the middle distance. Pony took a pull on the whiskey jug.

"What kinda help you need?" Virgil said.

"I know you come back to Appaloosa. I think you be the lawman here," Pony said.

Virgil nodded.

"Kha-to-nay kill an Indian agent and rob train," Pony said.

Without looking at us, Kha-to-nay said something in Apache. Pony answered. Kha-to-nay said something else. Pony nodded.

"Kha-to-nay say he not rob train. He destroy train. He say Chiricahua people at war with white-eyes. Say destroy train is act of war."

"How 'bout the Indian agent?" Virgil said.

"Kill white-eye . . . *tirano?*" Pony said, and looked at me.

"Tyrant," I said.

"Kill white-eye tyrant," Pony said. "Free Chiricahua people."

"So, the government is after him for the Indian agent," Virgil said. "And the Pinkertons are after him for the railroad."

"U.S. Marshals arrest Kha-to-nay," Pony said. "Put him in jail. I get him out. We come here."

"How'd you get him out of Yaqui?" Virgil said.

Pony smiled and patted his Colt. Virgil nodded.

"There a bounty on him?" Virgil said.

"*Sí,*" Pony said.

Virgil rocked back a little in his chair and took the jug from me and took a pull.

45

"Well," Virgil said. "We can't let 'em take you."

11

"You want to move in here?" Virgil said.

Pony shook his head.

"Kha-to-nay not stay with white devil," Pony said.

"Don't blame him," Virgil said. "Wasn't one myself I wouldn't stay with him, either."

"Not understand," Pony said.

"Virgil's making a joke," I said.

"Got any money?" Virgil said.

Pony smiled and nodded.

"When Kha-to-nay destroy train in war with white tyrant, he take money, too."

"Kha-to-nay's not so dumb," I said.

From his place at the far end of the porch Kha-to-nay said nothing.

"Anybody on your trail?" Virgil said.

Pony shook his head.

"Only man can track Pony Flores," he said, "is me."

"Good," Virgil said. "Police ain't on our side here."

"You on other side of law now?" Pony said.

"Neither side," Virgil said. "Just keeping order in the Boston House saloon."

"You not the law," Pony said. "Maybe we bring you trouble. Maybe should move on."

"Where?" Virgil said. "Here, you got two friends in town."

"Four," Allie said.

We all looked at her. Virgil nodded slowly.

"Four friends in town," he said.

Pony nodded.

"All good with gun," he said, and smiled at Laurel.

She almost smiled back.

"We stay," Pony said, "for while."

"Then what?" Allie said.

"We see," Pony said.

"See what?" Allie said.

Pony looked at Virgil.

"See what develops, Allie," Virgil said.

"That's your plan?" Allie said.

"Plan gonna depend on what develops," Virgil said.

"So, how do you know you can handle what develops?" Allie said.

Ladies, don't drink from the jug, I thought, *but they sometimes have several from the glass.*

"Don't," Virgil said.

"What about all of that stuff Everett talks

about from *Who's-he-which on War?*" Allie said.

"Clausewitz," I said. "Prepare for what your enemy can do, not what you think he will do."

"How about that?" Allie said to Virgil.

"Hell, Allie," Virgil said. "Don't know who the enemy is yet."

"So, you just wander into it," Allie said. "The great Virgil Cole, full of yourself, assuming, as you always do, that you can handle everything."

Virgil said, "Don't know how else to go, Allie."

"Everett's no better," Allie said. "You go, he goes, too."

She poured an unladylike slug of whiskey into her glass and drank some.

"Well, what about me? What happens to Laurel?" she said.

"Wouldn't have found Laurel without Pony," Virgil said.

Allie didn't say anything for a moment.

Then she said, "Men!" and shook her head.

Laurel looked as solemn as always.

12

A short, fat man with a goatee, wearing a flat-crowned black hat, came into the Boston House in the late afternoon with Lamar Speck. He and Speck located Virgil leaning on the bar.

"Virgil," Speck said. "This is Buford Posner."

Virgil nodded.

"I own the Golden Palace," Posner said, "down the street, and there's trouble there right now."

"I suggested you and Everett," Speck said. He was speaking very fast.

"Whaddya need?" Virgil said to Posner.

"A group of cowboys are causing trouble in my place," Posner said. "They've run off my lookout, and Lamar tells me you've been successful with this sort of thing in the past."

"Why not the police?" Virgil said.

"Like Lamar, I am not on good terms with the police," Posner said. "I will pay you, of course."

"Be a favor to me, Virgil," Speck said.

Virgil looked at me.

"Everett?"

"Why not," I said.

"They say they are going to destroy my saloon," Posner said.

"Then we better hurry," Virgil said. "Everett, bring your eight-gauge."

The Golden Palace wasn't much on the outside, but inside it was a fancy, fussy little place with murals painted on the walls and ornate plaster moldings. There were eight cowboys in there, drinking whiskey from the bottle. A couple were sitting on the bar, the rest at a pair of tables. The spittoons had been tipped over. There was broken glass on the floor, and someone had shot holes, kind of strategically, in the mural of a wood nymph.

Behind us, Posner said, "My God," and backed out the door. Virgil and I went in without him.

One of the cowboys looked at us as we pushed into the saloon and said, "Who the fuck are you?"

"Name's Virgil Cole," Virgil said. "Big fella with the siege gun is Everett Hitch."

"Want a drink?" the cowboy said.

He was young, probably no more than

twenty-five, and he wore a big Colt with a black handle in a low-cut holster tied down on his right thigh.

"No," Virgil said. "We'd like you boys to leave."

"Leave?" the young cowboy said.

I moved away from Virgil, so that I was close to the saloon wall on Virgil's right. He moved left, against the bar.

"Correct," Virgil said.

The young cowboy jumped down from the bar and faced Virgil.

"What happens if we don't leave?" he said.

"We shoot some of you," Virgil said.

I thumbed the hammers back on the eight-gauge. It was a touch of theater, the sound of the hammers snicking back. We'd done it a hundred times before. But I also knew that Virgil was ready to shoot. He didn't seem to have changed position, but I knew that he was balanced, knees bent a little, shoulders relaxed. He looked steadily at the young cowboy. It was a hard look to meet. But the young cowboy had the wild eyes you see sometimes in bucking horses, and he held the look. I knew Virgil didn't care if the kid held his look or not. Virgil was in the place he goes to when it might be time to shoot. Everything registered and nothing mattered.

"You gonna shoot all of us?" the kid said.

"Depends," Virgil said.

"On what?" the kid said.

The other cowboys had gathered behind him. All of them were heeled.

"On what you all do," Virgil said. "You pull on me and I'll kill you."

"All of us," the kid said.

"You first," Virgil said. "Everett will get some with the scatter gun. Then we'll see."

The kid looked around for a moment at the other cowboys.

"Wanna go at 'em?" he said.

Somebody behind him said, "Lazy L don't back down from nobody."

The kid nodded. He looked back at Virgil. He was going to try it.

You do this enough you can sense it. I knew he was going to try. Virgil knew. We maybe both knew before the kid really did.

The kid's shoulders twitched, and Virgil drew his gun and had the hammer back before the kid reached his holster. I had the eight-gauge at my shoulder. We were far enough apart so that they'd have to decide which of us to shoot at.

The kid froze with his fingertips on the black butt of his Colt.

"Jesus Christ," the kid said.

"Might want to back down from this one,"

Virgil said.

"How'd you do that?" the kid said.

"Done it before," Virgil said.

"For crissake, you didn't even move fast," the kid said.

"Fast enough," Virgil said.

The kid slowly moved his hand away from his gun.

"I'm really fast," the kid said.

The tension had gone out of the room.

"Sure," Virgil said.

"You coulda killed me easy," the kid said.

"Sure," Virgil said.

The kid started slowly toward the door. The other cowboys followed.

Virgil turned slowly as they moved. I did, too, with the shotgun still at my shoulder.

When they were gone, Virgil holstered his Colt. I lowered the eight-gauge.

"Lazy L," I said. "Could be General Laird's place."

"Could be," Virgil said.

"If it is," I said, "they might be getting tired of us."

"Might," Virgil said.

"If they are," I said, "I s'pose they'll let us know."

"Probably," Virgil said.

He found a couple of unbroken glasses on the bar and poured us each a drink. We were sipping it when the saloon doors opened a crack and Posner looked in.

"Everybody's gone?" he said.

"They are," Virgil said. "Care for a drink?"

13

It was raining, a nice, straight-down summer rain. We sat on the covered front porch after supper and drank coffee and watched it. Allie and Laurel were still cleaning up inside.

"What was that we ate for supper?" Virgil said.

"Dinner," I said. "Allie told me it's properly called dinner."

"Whatever we call it, it was heavy going," Virgil said.

"I think what we ate might once have been a tough old chicken," I said.

"Think it was," Virgil said. "But what was in the pot with it?"

"Don't know," I said. "Coffee ain't much, either."

"Gotta put a lot of sugar in it," Virgil said.

"Whiskey might help."

"Suspicion it would," Virgil said. "You got the jug over by you?"

"I do."

Virgil held his cup out toward me.

"Whyn't your pour a little into this coffee for me," Virgil said.

I poured some for both of us. The rain smelled very clean, and things seemed fresh.

"Kid in the saloon today," I said. "Was really interested in whether he could kill you."

Virgil nodded.

"Then when he couldn't, he was just as interested in why he couldn't," I said.

"Wants to be a pistolero," Virgil said.

"He needs to get better," I said.

"Does," Virgil said, and sipped from his cup.

Allie and Laurel came out of the house with coffee and sat down with us.

"You drinking whiskey in that coffee?" Allie said.

"We are," Virgil said. "Hard to drink it without some."

"Oh, Virgil," she said. "You know you don't mean it."

Virgil looked at me.

" 'Course he don't," I said.

"Everett," Allie said. "You might pour a splash for me and Laurel."

I poured some into Allie's coffee.

"Go easy on the child," Allie said.

57

"Sure," I said.

"I met Mrs. Callico this afternoon, at a church meeting. A fine lady. Educated back east. Very good manners."

"Like you," Virgil said.

"Oh, Virgil, you know I don't have an eastern education," Allie said.

"You're a fine lady, anyway," Virgil said.

"Oh, Virgil," she said. "That's so sweet."

Virgil smiled. The rain was making the soft noise rain can make, when it's right.

"What are you going to do about Pony?" Allie said.

"Nothing," Virgil said.

"I think you should tell him to move on," Allie said.

"Thought he had four friends here," Virgil said.

"Of course he does, Virgil. But he's trouble," Allie said. "For all of us. I think you should tell him."

"Ain't gonna do that, Allie," Virgil said.

"It's not him so much," Allie said. "It's that brother. I don't like him. I don't like the way he looks at me. And you know Laurel and Indians. Poor child won't even look at him."

"Ain't afraid of Pony," Virgil said.

"He ain't all Indian," Allie said.

Virgil stood and walked to Laurel's chair.

"You afraid of Kha-to-nay?" Virgil said, and bent down to her.

She whispered in his ear. He nodded and whispered back to her. She whispered again. Virgil smiled.

"Says she is scared of Kha-to-nay," he said. "But she knows Pony won't let him hurt her."

"Mrs. Callico invited me to have tea with her sometime," Allie said.

"That's nice," Virgil said.

"We live here," Allie said. "We own a house. It is my chance to have a regular life, Virgil."

"Sure," Virgil said. "I want that for you, Allie."

"Then get rid of Pony," she said. "And his brother."

Virgil shook his head. Laurel made a sound. All of us looked at her. It might have been the first sound she'd made since we got her. She made the sound again and shook her head violently.

Allie began to cry.

"Nobody understands," she said. "Nobody understands me."

"We do," Virgil said. "All of us know you want to be a fine churchgoing lady. And all of us know that being friendly with a breed

59

carries a knife in his moccasin don't help that."

Allie looked up with tears on her face.

"Then send him away," Allie said.

Laurel made her noise again.

"Can't," Virgil said.

Allie stood with her hands covering her face and her shoulders shaking, and rushed into the house.

Virgil looked at me silently for a minute.

Then he said, "Know them long walks we was talking about you and Laurel taking?"

"I do," I said.

"Don't think there'll be so much need for 'em right now," Virgil said.

14

It was morning. There was a CLOSED sign on the door to the Boston House saloon. Virgil and I sat at a big round table in the back of the saloon. With us sat Lamar Speck, Buford Posner, and five other men. The room was otherwise empty. Except for Willis McDonough, who was setting up the bar. Outside, the rain that had made things fresh yesterday was making things soggy today.

"This is a private meeting," Speck said. "What we talk about here doesn't leave the room. Anybody don't understand that?"

Nobody said they didn't.

"This here's Virgil Cole and Everett Hitch," Speck said. "You all know who they are and what they do. They done it for me, and you know what happened at Buford's place this week.

"Boys," Speck continued, "everybody at the table owns a saloon, or similar public place. Buford, you know, owns the Golden Palace."

He introduced us around the table, and identified each man with his business.

"All us got the same problem," Speck said. "And we thought you boys might be able to help us."

Speck shifted in his chair and studied the backs of his hands for a moment. Virgil and I waited.

"It's Callico," Speck said.

He looked around the table. No one fainted. Speck glanced at the front door of the saloon. No one came in.

"He charges something he calls a 'safeguard fee.' We pay him regular, and when there's trouble the police will come at once and put things right."

"And if you don't pay him regular?" Virgil said.

"They don't come," Speck said.

Virgil looked at me and smiled faintly.

"Fee a big one?" I said.

"Substantial," Speck said.

"Thinking you could get the same service for less?" I said.

"Yes," Speck said. "We been talking 'bout that, seein' as you boys done it twice already."

" 'Cause you wouldn't pay Callico's safeguard money," Virgil said.

"Yes, Buford and I agreed it was extortion, and refused to pay."

"Which is why you had to hire us when Nicky Laird run off your shotgun lookout."

"Yes. And it's why I brought Buford to you. And it's why all of us are here now. We all chip in. We post them rules of yours in our establishments. You'll be here, and if there's any trouble anyplace, they'll send for you, and you come running. We get safety. You get money."

"There enough trouble?" Virgil said. "We come cheaper than Callico. But we ain't cheap."

"We'll guarantee you a year," Speck said. "There's enough trouble. More since you left. More since the police stopped showing up. And more as the town gets bigger. And more since General Laird took over Bragg's place."

"He the Lazy L?" I said.

"He is," Speck said. "But Nicky mostly runs it."

"Couple things to think about," Virgil said.

"I know we can meet your price," Speck said.

Everybody at the table agreed.

"Good," Virgil said. " 'Nother thing is, Everett and me do this, sooner or later we gonna have to kill somebody."

Nobody said anything.

"Anybody care 'bout that?" Virgil said.

Speck looked at the other men around the table, then at Virgil. No one appeared to care.

"You boys should do what you need to do," he said.

Virgil nodded slowly and looked at me.

"Everett?" he said.

"Not like we got something else to do," I said.

Virgil kept nodding. He looked back at Speck.

"Okay," he said.

Later we sat on the front porch of the Boston House admiring the rainwashed air.

"Smells nice after it rains," Virgil said.

"Um-hm."

Virgil tilted his chair onto its back two legs and allowed it to balance there, its back resting against the hotel wall.

"You thinking?" he said.

"Yep."

" 'Bout Callico?" Virgil said.

"Yep."

Virgil nodded. He allowed the chair to rock slightly on its rear legs, the back tapping lightly against the wall.

"Me, too," he said.

"Ain't gonna like us taking away his safeguard business," I said.

"True," Virgil said.

"We kill somebody, be his chance to come after us."

"Might," Virgil said.

"Other hand," I said. "If Stringer's right, Callico's after bigger things when statehood comes."

"So, he might not want to open up the fee question," Virgil said.

"Might not," I said.

"Guess we just proceed," Virgil said. "See what comes along."

15

Virgil and I took to sitting out on the porch in front of the Boston House, the way we used to sit on the porch outside the jail, when we were the law in Appaloosa. Mostly we sat and watched the life on Main Street. It was handy to everybody we were supposed to be protecting. It was pleasant, especially since Appaloosa hadn't been all that rambunctious since we signed on. And now and then, Tilda would come out of the saloon to pour us some coffee.

"Appears to be a parade," Virgil said.

I looked down Main Street and saw Amos Callico coming up the street with six policemen carrying Winchesters. The policemen stopped in the street and formed a semicircle facing Virgil and me.

"No drum," I said to Virgil.

"Too bad," Virgil said.

Callico came up the steps and sat next to Virgil on the porch.

"You boys are costing me money," he said softly.

"I believe we are," Virgil said.

"I want it back," Callico said.

"I would, too," Virgil said. "I was you."

"I want you boys gone by Sunday," Callico said.

Virgil shook his head.

"You're telling me *no?*" Callico said.

"I am," Virgil said.

"You're here after Sunday, we'll kill you first time we see you."

"That sound legal to you, Everett?" Virgil said.

"Don't," I said.

"I'm the law in this town," Callico said. "If I do it, it's legal."

"Might cause you a little trouble down the line," Virgil said. "Sheriff's bound to look into it. Most likely it'll be Stringer, and he don't like you much, anyway."

"Fuck Stringer," Callico said.

"Everett," Virgil said. "You think shooting a couple of famous lawmen would look good, if you was gonna run for sheriff, or gov'nor, or God, or something?"

"Might not," I said.

Callico looked silently at both of us.

Then he said, "You may have a point there, Virgil. Maybe there's some way we can work this out more amicably."

Virgil looked at me.

" 'Amicably'?" he said.

"Friendly," I said.

"Not sure how amicable you and me can be, Amos," Virgil said.

Callico looked at the six policemen in the street. They were far enough away so that they couldn't hear what was being quietly spoken. He took a deep breath.

"There's a nice life to be lived here. Pleasant, respectable, and money to be made. There's enough for both of us. But not if we're on opposite sides. I've just started to develop this arrangement, and there's a lot more of it to come. If you just get out of the way. I'll give you a piece of it."

"How big a piece?" Virgil said.

"We can negotiate that," Callico said. "Be a percentage, I would think. So, as I grow you get more."

"You're planning on growing," Virgil said.

"I plan on owning this town," Callico said. "Every goddamned citizen will be giving me money regular."

"Got it all planned out?" Virgil said.

"I'm feelin' my way along. But it can be done."

" 'Less we get in your way."

"You're right," Callico said. "Be harder

for me if I have to kill you. But if it gets even harder when I don't kill you . . ."

Callico spread his hands, and raised his eyebrows, and shrugged.

"Don't need an answer right now, Virgil," Callico said. "Both you boys think on it."

"Be glad to," Virgil said.

"Be needing an answer by Sunday," Callico said.

"Surely," Virgil said.

We all sat for a moment. Then Callico stood, nodded to us, and headed back down Main Street. His men followed. Virgil and I sat quiet for a time, and then Virgil spoke.

"You know," Virgil said. "Last time we was here we was lawmen. Now we appear to be outlaws."

"I guess," I said.

"Don't seem much different," Virgil said.

"Maybe it ain't," I said.

"Oughta be," Virgil said.

I shrugged.

"We gonna take his offer?" I said.

"No."

"We leaving town?"

"No."

"We gonna face it out with him?"

"Be my plan," Virgil said.

I nodded.

"Why don't we take his offer?"

"Don't like the man," Virgil said.

"Least you got a nice, strong reason," I said.

"Don't like him," Virgil said.

16

Pony had breakfast with us at Café Paris on Friday. The Chinaman who ran the café had some chickens, and they had been laying recently. So, with our beans and salt pork and biscuits, we each had an egg.

"Sick of cooking for me and Kha-to-nay," Pony said.

"How is life out on the prairie," I said.

Pony shrugged.

"Quiet," he said. "But Kha-to-nay wants to go back to war with white-eyes."

"Ain't gonna win that," I said.

"I know," Pony said. "Try to keep him alive long as I can. Balloon go up here on Sunday?"

Virgil shook his head.

"No?" I said.

Virgil shook his head again.

"He backed off the shooting," Virgil said. "Soon's we brought it up."

"Scared?" Pony said.

Virgil shook his head.

"Ambitious," he said.

"Afraid it would spoil his plan to be governor?" I said.

"Yep."

"He did shift the tone of the conversation," I said.

"He tell you go," Pony said. "He tell you, you not go he kill you."

"True," Virgil said. "But he won't."

"Think I come in town, anyway," Pony said. "Stay with you Sunday."

" 'Preciate it," Virgil said. "But I ain't wrong 'bout this."

"Wants to be known as the man who cleaned up Appaloosa," I said.

"Yep," Virgil said. "And he won't get that reputation by shooting us."

"Who actually did clean up Appaloosa," I said.

"Maybe for a while," Virgil said. "But Callico's a politician. Don't care nothing about actually."

"He lie?" Pony said.

"How he knows he's a politician," Virgil said.

17

Pony walked with us up from Café Paris and sat with us in our spot in front of the Boston House. Tilda brought us out some coffee.

"This what you do every day?" Pony said.

"When we ain't keeping order in our saloons," I said.

"How much you do that?" Pony said.

"Not so much," Virgil said.

"Mostly we do it from here. Anybody needs us, they send somebody."

"Don't seem too dangerous here," Pony said.

"Don't," Virgil said.

"Seem boring," Pony said.

"Is," Virgil said. "Mostly."

"Good for ladies," Pony said.

"Yep."

"How is Chiquita?" Pony said.

"Doin' fine," Virgil said. He was watching four horsemen come up the street. All four wore dusters and black Stetsons.

"Hello," I said.

Virgil nodded. Pony said nothing.

As the riders came abreast of us, they wheeled the horses and stopped in front of us.

"Looking for the police office in town," one of the riders said. He had very pale blue eyes and a thick mustache peppered with gray.

I told him where it was.

"Chief's name is Callico," I said.

The man was eyeing Virgil.

"Ain't you Virgil Cole?" the man said.

"I am," Virgil said.

"Seen you in Abilene," he said. "You were good."

Virgil grinned.

"Still am," he said.

"You the law here?" the man said.

"Nope," Virgil said. "Just a citizen."

"Dell Garrison," the man said. "I'm with the Pinkerton Detective Agency. We're chasing an Indian. Run off from the Apache reservation. Held up a train. Killed a couple railroad employees."

"What makes you think he's here?" Virgil said.

"Folks in Van Buren spotted them, couple

weeks back, heading south. This is the next town."

Virgil nodded.

Garrison looked at Pony.

"He's traveling with a breed," Garrison said.

"Know the breed's name?" Virgil said.

"Nope."

"How 'bout the Indian?" Virgil said.

"Got it wrote down somewhere in my saddlebags," Garrison said. "Indian name."

Garrison looked at Pony some more.

"You a breed?" he said to Pony.

Pony said something in Spanish.

"He a friend of yours?" Garrison said.

"He is," Virgil said.

"What'd he say?"

"Don't know," Virgil said. "Don't speak Spanish. Everett, you know what he said?"

"No," I said.

"You're Everett Hitch," Garrison said.

"Yep."

"Breed speak any English?"

"Never heard him," I said.

"This fella's a friend and you don't speak Spanish and he don't speak English."

"We're pretty quiet," I said.

"He a breed?" Garrison said.

"Don't know," Virgil said.

Garrison nodded and looked at me.

"That an eight-gauge?" he said.

"It is," I said.

"Don't see them much," Garrison said. "Wells Fargo issues them, I think."

"That's where I got it," I said.

Garrison looked at Pony some more. Pony said nothing, showed nothing.

"You see my Indian," Garrison said, "or the breed he's running with, the railroad's got a nice reward out."

"Bounty hunters?" I said. "Sure . . . big reward."

"They following you?" Virgil said.

Garrison smiled.

"You know the trade," he said. "Yeah, they let us do the finding and then try to slip in ahead of us and get there first."

"You mind?" I said.

"We get paid either way, and we ain't eligible for the reward, anyway."

"Dead or alive?" Virgil said.

"Yep."

"Dead is easier," Virgil said.

"Yep," Garrison said. "And, hell, he's an Indian."

Nobody said anything.

"Well," Garrison said. "Keep an eye out."

"Surely will," Virgil said.

Garrison backed his horse out a couple of steps away from us and turned him and

76

headed on down toward Callico's office. The three other riders followed.

When they were gone, Virgil turned to Pony.

"Place up north a ways, Resolution. Me and Everett worked there a while back. Last I knew, the law up there was a couple boys we worked with."

"Cato Tillson," I said. "And Frank Rose."

"You tell 'em we sent you," Virgil said. "Be a nice place to hunker down for a while."

"What about police chief?" Pony said. "Sunday."

"Callico?" Virgil said. "On Sunday, Callico's gonna let it slide."

"You know?"

"Know enough," Virgil said. "Don't worry about Callico."

Pony nodded slowly.

"We will go there," Pony said.

Pony smiled and shrugged.

"I was Garrison," Virgil said, "I'd turn that corner and send a man back along Front Street to see what you done. If you lit out, I'd have him follow you."

"Ain't going to light out," Pony said. "Go home with you."

Virgil nodded.

Pony smiled.

"Then light out," he said.

"I was you," Virgil said, "and I was gonna light out anyway, I'd collect Kha-to-nay and light out 'fore Allie cooked you supper."

"*Sí,*" Pony said.

"And tell your brother," I said, "not to irritate Cato."

"*Sí,*" Pony said.

Then the three of us got up and walked down Main Street toward Virgil's house.

18

On Sunday morning Virgil was sitting where he sat, in front of the Boston House. He was heeled and his Winchester leaned against the wall beside his chair. I was across the street with the eight-gauge, standing on the boardwalk in the shade in front of the feed store. Above us the sky was a pale, even, uninterrupted blue that appeared to stretch clear west at least to California.

People were on the street, dressed up, the women especially, going to church. I saw Allie go by in her best dress, with Laurel. They were walking with a tall, handsome woman in clothes that looked like she'd shopped in New York. Allie waved at Virgil as she passed. Virgil touched the brim of his hat.

We waited. That was okay. We were good at it. Virgil and I could wait as long as we needed to. Around midday, Callico came down the street with his Winchester escorts.

They stopped in front of Virgil. Callico looked around, saw me across the street, and murmured something to his escort. Three of the policemen turned and faced me. I nodded at them. Nobody nodded back.

"I've decided not to kill you, Virgil," Callico said.

He had a big voice, and it carried easily from the Boston House to the feed store.

Virgil looked at the armed policemen.

"You ever go anyplace alone, Amos?" Virgil said.

"I'm not a violent man," Callico said. "And I figure it's easier to get along with you than kill both of you."

"A sight easier," Virgil said.

"Long as you don't break the law," Callico said.

Virgil didn't comment.

"And I'll be keeping my eye on you," Callico said.

"Expect you will," Virgil said.

"You break a law and I'll come down on you like an avalanche."

"Avalanche," Virgil said.

"Like a mountain fell on you," Callico said.

Virgil nodded.

"Amos," he said. "You got to stop trying

to scare us. Ain't effective. Me 'n Everett been doin' gun work too long."

"This is a small town," Callico said. "And a big country. I'm not going to sacrifice the big for the small, you understand that?"

"Surely do," Virgil said.

"So, you do your business, and I'll do mine, and you stay clean, we won't bother each other."

"That sounds fine," Virgil said.

He raised his voice.

"That sound fine to you, Everett?" he said.

"Fine," I said.

"We think it's fine," Virgil said.

Callico looked at Virgil for a considerable time without a sound.

Then he said, "Mind your step, Virgil. Just mind your step."

He turned and led his policemen on down the street. I strolled over to where Virgil was and sat down beside him.

"Pompous son of a bitch," I said.

"Don't mean he ain't good with a Colt," Virgil said.

"Stringer claims he's one of the best," I said.

"Stringer knows something about that," Virgil said.

"On the other hand, we're pretty good, too," I said.

81

"We are," Virgil said. "Ain't we."

Tilda came out with coffee and we settled in for another day.

19

Allie and Laurel liked to walk up Main Street in the evening, but Laurel wouldn't leave the house without Virgil, so when they wanted to go, we went, too, and strolled with them past the dress shop window, where Allie told Laurel how beautiful the clothes were. Laurel stared at them silently.

At the end of Main Street, past Seventh, were the short-time whorehouses, so we stopped before we reached them, and crossed the street and headed back down along Main Street. Walking ahead with Virgil, Laurel would pause sometimes and whisper to him. Allie and I dropped a few steps behind.

"You think she'll ever talk to me, Everett?" Allie said.

"Might," I said.

"I've been a mother to her since what happened," Allie said.

"You've been a good one, Allie."

"I guess she talks to Virgil because he saved her," Allie said.

"I saved her, too," I said. "And she won't talk to me."

"Or Pony Flores," Allie said. "Virgil always says you wouldn't have found her without Pony Flores."

"True," I said.

"She even hugs him, but doesn't speak."

"I know," I said.

"There must be something about Virgil," she said.

"Virgil's not like other people, Allie."

"No," she said. "He certainly isn't."

We passed the Golden Palace. The light and sound spilled gladly out onto the street.

"Everything seems so peaceful now," Allie said.

"Yes."

"Did Virgil ask Pony to leave?" Allie said.

"Pinkertons showed up looking for him," I said. "We sent them up to Resolution. Know the law there."

"Resolution was where you and Virgil were for a time, while I was . . . away."

"Yes," I said.

"Why doesn't Kha-to-nay go back to his people?" Allie said.

"First place they'd look for him," I said. "And Pony is afraid that if he's back with the tribe he'll instigate trouble."

"So, it wasn't because I asked him," Allie said.

We passed the Boston House.

"How are things with the police chief," Allie said.

"Fine."

"Mrs. Callico invited me and Laurel to tea after church last Sunday," Allie said. "She's so elegant. From New Orleans."

"Never been to New Orleans," I said.

"And she speaks French," Allie said.

Ahead of us, Virgil walked with a slight forward bend, so he could listen when Laurel whispered to him.

"And she has clothes sent to her from there," Allie said.

We reached First Street and turned right on it, toward Front Street.

"And she has a Mexican woman who cooks and serves," Allie said.

"Can see why Callico needs income," I said.

"Oh, he's going to be very wealthy," Allie said.

"You're sure?"

"Mrs. Callico says he has a plan worked out. He'll get elected sheriff next year. And then, later, he'll go to Congress and come back and be a governor, and he says one day he'll be President."

"Of the country?" I said.

"That's what Mrs. Callico told me."

"The United States of America," I said.

"President of the United States," Allie said.

"Amos Callico," I said.

"Wouldn't that be exciting if he was, and we knew him?"

"Why would anybody want to be President?" I said.

"Oh, Everett," Allie said. "Don't be so silly."

20

Every couple of hours, more often at night, Virgil or I toured the saloons we were hired to protect. The one not touring would be in place in front of the Boston House in case there was trouble and someone sent for us. On a pleasant evening, with a lot of starlight, I was on tour. As I came out of the Sweet Water Saloon, Tilda, the Boston House waitress, came running.

"Trouble," she said. "Come fast."

"Boston House?" I said.

"Yes."

I went up Main Street at a run, carrying the eight-gauge.

In the Boston House, Virgil was in the doorway that led to the hotel lobby. He was leaning his left shoulder against the jamb. Standing across the room, with a half dozen of his ranch hands behind him, Nicky Laird was drunk. So were the hands.

"Sign says no guns," Nicky said to Virgil.

"Does," Virgil said.

"We got guns."

"Yeah, you do," Virgil said.

"Gonna try to do something 'bout that?" Nicky said.

"Have to ask you to leave," Virgil said.

"We ain't goin'," Nicky said.

"Then I have to disarm you."

"All seven of us?" Nicky said.

"Yep."

"Even if you got a round under the hammer," Nicky said. "You only got six."

"Three choices," Virgil said. "You leave, you take off the guns, or you pull on me. Anybody pulls on me, I kill you, too."

Behind Nicky I thumbed both hammers back on the eight-gauge. It was a loud sound in the quiet room. Several patrons silently moved out of the line of fire.

Nicky glanced back at me.

"Your back-shooting friend," he said to Virgil.

Virgil didn't answer.

"Don't change nothing," Nicky said.

Virgil nodded gently. His shoulders were relaxed. He seemed almost a little bored.

"The Laird name gets respect," Nicky said. "And if it don't, somebody pays hell for it."

"No reason it has to be you," Virgil said.

"Man's right," one of the hands said. "The general won't like this."

"Fuck the general," Nicky said. "I run things."

"You're a boy," Virgil said. "And you're drunk. I'll take no pride in killing you."

"Fuck you, too," Nicky said, and went for his gun.

Virgil shot him and a man on either side of him before anyone cleared leather. Everyone else froze. I didn't even have to shoot.

Someone said, "Jesus!"

"You boys leave the saloon," Virgil said, "and take them three with you."

The four men did as they were told. No one looked at Virgil or me. I let the hammers down on the eight-gauge. Virgil carefully took the spent shells from his Colt and fed in three fresh ones.

"Kid had choices," Virgil said.

"Had three," I said.

"Took the wrong one," Virgil said.

"Kinda thought he would," I said.

"Drunk," Virgil said.

"And young," I said.

"Too young," Virgil said.

"Maybe," I said. "But old enough to kill you, if you let him."

" 'Fraid so," Virgil said.

89

21

When we could, Virgil liked to take the horses out and run them so's to keep their wind good. On Sunday morning, while Allie and Laurel were in church, we were in the hills back of Bragg's old spread, which was now the Lazy L.

The Appaloosa stallion was still there with his mares. He looked at us, stiff-legged, as we sat our horses on the west flank of a hill. He tossed his head.

"Smells the geldings," I said.

"Stallions don't like geldings," Virgil said.

"Wonder why?" I said. "Ain't no competition."

"Maybe he don't know that," Virgil said.

"But you and I both seen a stallion attack a gelding without no mares around. Gelding minding his own business."

"Maybe the stud just don't like the idea of geldings," Virgil said.

"Can't say I'm all that fond of it myself," I said.

"Probably don't smell like a mare," Virgil said. "And don't smell like a stallion, and he don't know what it is."

"Creatures don't seem to like things they don't know what it is," I said.

The stallion moved nervously around his herd of mares. Head up, tail up, ears forward. One of the mares was cropping grass a few feet away, separate from the herd. The stallion nipped her on the flank, and she closed with the other mares.

"Stays right around here," Virgil said.

"Why you suppose he keeps them here?" I said. "Lotta herds drift."

"Good grass," Virgil said. "Water, lotta shelter in the winter."

"Not much competition, I'd guess."

"I dunno, see a couple new scars on him," Virgil said. "One on his neck there, and one on his left shoulder."

"Could be wolves," I said.

"Looks like horse to me," Virgil said.

"Ain't seen no other wild horses around here," I said.

"Maybe somebody rides a stud," Virgil said. "And it wandered."

"Lotta work being a stud," I said.

"It is," Virgil said.

"Gets a lot of humping," I said.

"Wonder if it's worth it," Virgil said.

"He keeps at it," I said.

Another mare strayed, and the stallion dashed around the herd with his head low and his neck out flat, and drove her back.

"Worth it to him, I guess," Virgil said.

22

The funeral for Nicky Laird was held on Monday morning. Virgil and I watched the procession from the window of Café Paris, where we were eating fried salt pork and biscuits and all four of the eggs the China-man had that day.

The Appaloosa police force in full uniform marched behind the hearse, and Chief Cal-lico sat in the black funeral carriage with a starchy-looking old man who was probably General Laird.

"Callico appears to be a friend of the fam-ily," I said.

"Seems so," Virgil said.

There was a sturdy-looking Mexican woman in the carriage, too. She was crying.

"Not the mother," I said. "The general didn't marry no Mexican."

Virgil shook his head.

"Don't see no mother," Virgil said.

"Probably the housekeeper," I said.

"Maybe raised the boy."

"Must be hard burying a child," Virgil said.

"Must be," I said.

"Got no children, so I guess we can't know," Virgil said.

"Got Laurel," I said.

"Be hard burying Laurel," Virgil said.

"Would," I said.

We drank our coffee. The funeral proceeded past.

"You had to kill him, Virgil," I said. "Don't see what else you coulda done."

Virgil nodded.

"Killing don't bother me," Virgil said. "Long as I follow the rules."

"You gave him a choice," I said.

"He's got to know what he's up against," Virgil said. "He's got to have a chance to walk away."

"He knew who you were. He was looking for a fight. He coulda chosen not to fight," I said.

"He could," Virgil said.

"That one of the rules?" I said.

Virgil always seemed clear on the rules, but I never exactly knew how the rules got made.

"Sometimes," Virgil said.

"How 'bout the five men had Laurel and

her mother," I said. "Didn't give them no chance."

"The rule there was *save the women,*" Virgil said.

"How 'bout if somebody shoots first," I said.

Virgil grinned.

"Rule there is *save your ass,*" he said.

"So, the rules change," I said.

" 'Course they do," Virgil said. "Ain't no one rule for everything."

I said, "Which means sometimes you have to make one up pretty quick."

"Sometimes the fight makes the rules for you," Virgil said. "And you only know afterwards that it was a rule at all."

"You do have some ideas," I said. "You reading books again?"

"Still reading this Emerson fella," Virgil said. "Mostly it's mush, but sometimes he says something."

"Say much about gunfight rules?" I said.

"Ain't touched on that, so far," Virgil said.

"How 'bout that drummer you shot, the one run off with Allie?"

"I broke the rules," Virgil said.

"You shot him 'cause you were mad," I said.

"I did. He hadn't broken no law."

"And you were the law," I said.

"Yep."

"So, the law was the rule then," I said.

"Yep."

"But now we ain't the law," I said.

"Hell," Virgil said. "We're on the other side of the law in this town."

"But there's still rules," I said.

" 'Course there are," Virgil said. "Don't you got any rules, Everett?"

"Don't think much about it," I said. "Mostly I just follow yours."

Virgil smiled slightly and looked at me silently for a while.

Then he said, "Good."

23

Virgil and I were thinking about lunch, and fearing that Allie would bring some, when a man on a tall gray horse rode alone up Main Street and stopped in front of the Boston House, where Virgil and I were sitting. He was a tall man, barrel-bodied, with a white beard and thick white hair, under the kind of gray slouch hat that Confederate cavalry officers used to wear.

"I'm Horatio Laird," he said to Virgil. "You killed my son."

"I'm sorry about that, sir," Virgil said. "He left me no choice."

"I know you," Laird said. "You're a professional killer. My son was wild, but he was no gunfighter."

"He was drunk, sir," Virgil said. "He pulled on me."

"He didn't have a chance," Laird said.

"He did," Virgil said. "I gave him one. He didn't take it."

"He was a proud boy," General Laird said. "Hotheaded, never a boy to back down."

Virgil nodded. The general's voice thickened.

"I . . . I taught him that," he said.

Neither Virgil nor I said anything.

"God help me," the general said.

His big-boned gray was a stallion, with a black mane and tail. I wondered if he was the one that had been after the Appaloosa's mares. He was so big a horse that the general was high above us, the reins slack over the saddle horn, hands folded on top of them, the knuckles white with effort. He didn't seem to be carrying a weapon.

"He thought he was faster than he was, sir," Virgil said.

The general was shaking his head slowly left, right, left, right.

"Wasn't me," Virgil said. "It was gonna be somebody."

"He died standing up," I said. "Facing the man who killed him."

"You . . . think . . . that matters . . . to . . . me?" the general said.

"No, sir," Virgil said. "Probably don't. But there ain't much else to say."

He shook his head some more. Left, right. Left, right.

"My son's dead, Cole, and you're not,"

the general said. "That ain't right."

He seemed to be having trouble with his breath.

"I could, I'd kill you where you're sitting. But you're too fast."

His breath was harsh.

"But I'll make it happen," he rasped, "if I have to shoot you in the back."

Nobody spoke. The general struggled with his breath for a moment, and then wheeled the stallion and rode off down the street.

"Think he means it?" I said.

"Not about shooting me in the back," Virgil said. "I expect he can't. Man like him. Be against the rules."

"Those rules again," I said.

"He pretty surely got more than I do," Virgil said. "He'll find another way."

"Hire somebody?" I said.

"S'pect he might," Virgil said.

24

Chief Callico stopped by our place of business, outside the Boston House, where Virgil and I were looking at the town and drinking coffee. He sat with us. He was neighborly Amos today.

"By God, Virgil," he said. "You've put me in a bind."

"Weren't my intention," Virgil said.

He sipped his coffee and looked over the rim of the mug past the rooftops of the town, at the higher country to the west. The land was mostly brown, with some moments of green, where there was water.

"Horatio Laird is the most important man in this part of the country," Callico said.

"I believe he is," Virgil said.

"Did you have to kill his only son?" Callico said.

"I did," Virgil said.

"He's pressing me real hard about it," Callico said.

"Wants me arrested," Virgil said.

"He wants that very bad," Callico said.

"Can't say I blame him," Virgil said.

Tilda came out with a pot of coffee and poured some for us.

"Tilda," Virgil said. "Why don't you get a cup for our friend Amos here."

"Yessir, Mr. Cole," Tilda said.

"But we both know I can't arrest you," Callico said.

He took the cup from Tilda and held it while she poured.

"You got fifty eyewitnesses that it was self-defense," Callico said.

"Didn't know it was that many," Virgil said. "You know that, Everett?"

"Knew there were enough," I said.

"I got plans," Callico said. "I'm trying to enforce the law in this town, and do it in a way will help me with those plans, you understand?"

"Heard you was aiming for president," Virgil said.

"And, by God, I'd be a good one, Virgil," Callico said. "But there's some stops 'fore we get there. And I got to make them."

"And you don't get to make them," I said, "arresting people and having to turn them loose."

"Correct. And I don't make them unless I

enforce the law right," Callico said. "And I don't make them unless I got support from important people, like General Laird."

"And right now you're in a squeeze," I said.

"You see that," Callico said.

Virgil drank some more coffee.

"Everett went to West Point," he said.

"Smart fella," Callico said. "Both of you are smart fellas. You give me any support you can, I'll appreciate it, and I'll remember it when I've made a few of those stops."

"Need money to go where you want to go," Virgil said.

"Sure do," Callico said. "One reason people like the general are important."

"Reason why you charge folks a fee for police services, too," Virgil said.

"Town don't give us enough operating budget," Callico said. "Got to do what I can."

Callico smiled a big, friendly smile.

"Opened up a little business for you boys, too," he said.

Virgil nodded.

"Did," he said.

"I can do things like that," Callico said.

Virgil and I didn't say anything.

"I ain't asking you boys for help. You're the only ones round here could give me trouble. You stay out of my way, and I'll consider it help."

"We got no ill will," Virgil said. "Do we, Everett."

"Nope."

"Good," Callico said. "Thanks for the coffee."

He stood and walked back down Main Street.

I looked at Virgil.

"You sure we don't have no ill will?" I said.

Still studying the western horizon, Virgil smiled slowly.

"Well," he said. "Maybe a little."

25

I had started keeping company with Emma Scarlet.

"Your partner killed General Laird's son," Emma said.

It was midafternoon and business was slow for both of us, so we took a siesta in her room.

"Yes," I said.

"And I started it," Emma said.

"I guess," I said.

"It'll get him in trouble with the general," Emma said.

"Or it might get the general in trouble with Virgil," I said.

The life hadn't gotten her yet, and she still looked pretty good with her clothes off.

"General draws an awful lot of water, round here," Emma said.

"I heard that," I said.

"Be governor if he hadn't been a reb," Emma said.

"People still care?" I said.

"Not around here," she said. "But lot of other voters. Don't make much difference to me. I can't vote, anyhow."

"What you can do, though, you do pretty well," I said.

"Pretty well?" she said.

"Best in the history of the goddamned world," I said.

She giggled.

"Oh, Everett," she said. "That's real sweet."

"Like me," I said.

"Most men are scared of the general," she said.

"Virgil ain't," I said.

"How do you know so sure?" Emma said.

" 'Cause Virgil ain't scared of anything," I said.

"I feel kinda bad about Nicky getting killed," Emma said. "You know? Like it was my fault. Couldn't Virgil have just whonked him on the head with his gun?"

"Ever see a gunfight, Emma?"

"Sure, I have. I'm a whore. I work saloons. Seen a lot. Drunks, mostly. Usually they miss."

"There's another kind, too," I said.

"Like the ones you and Virgil do?"

"Like those," I said. "What I learned

about those, I learned from Virgil. Because of what he does, what we do, mostly we're outnumbered."

"Like you were with Nicky," Emma said.

"Yep. So we got to mean it, soon as it starts. No whonking people. No shooting them in the leg. They need to know, and we need to know, that we are ready to kill them."

"Someone told me Nicky had six men with him," Emma said. "How come they all didn't just start shooting at the same time and kill both of you."

"Couple reasons," I said. "One, Virgil always makes it one against one. He always lets them know that if they draw first they are going to die first. And he's so quick that he's killed the first man before anyone else has cleared the holster. It tends to freeze everyone. Once they freeze, it's over."

"God," Emma said. "You talk about this like it was some kind of regular work, like herding cows."

"Seems like regular work after a while, I guess. How 'bout you?"

Emma giggled.

"Depends who I have to fuck," Emma said.

"It would," I said. "Wouldn't it."

"I do it 'cause, pretty much, I gotta. I got

106

no money, no husband, don't know how to do nothing else," Emma said. "But you can do other stuff. You don't have to do what you do. You been to the United States Military Academy. How come you just do gun work."

"Me and Virgil," I said. "We're good at it. Hell, Virgil may be the best there is at it."

"And you like that."

"It's pleasing," I said. "To be good at what you do."

"You like killing folks," Emma said.

I thought about that for a while.

"Not so much killing," I said. "But when we do it, and, Virgil would say, do it right, it's like we say, *This is us; this is who we are; this is what we do.*"

"And you like that."

"Guess we do," I said.

"You think I'm good at what I do?" Emma said.

"Best in history," I said.

"Want me to do it again?"

"One's all I can afford," I said.

Emma rolled over on top of me.

"On the house," she said.

26

Nicky Laird had been dead for three weeks. I was in the Golden Palace explaining to a very drunk mule skinner why he couldn't buy more whiskey on credit. He was kind of stubborn about it, so I hit him in the stomach with the butt of the eight-gauge and threw him off the front steps into Third Street.

I came back into the saloon, and a man came in behind me. He was wearing a beaded buckskin shirt, an ivory-handled Colt on his hip, and a derby hat tilted forward over the bridge of his nose. He looked like somebody from a wild west show, except, somehow, I knew he wasn't.

"Nicely done," the man said to me.

He had black-and-white striped pants tucked into high black boots, and his skin was smooth and kind of pale, like a woman's. He didn't look like he spent much time outside. His hands were pale, too, with long fingers.

"No guns," I said, "allowed in the saloon."

"Oh," he said. "Of course. Perhaps we could step out onto the veranda."

First time I ever heard it called a veranda. But we stepped out onto it anyway.

"No wasted movement," he said when we were outside.

"Thanks," I said.

"Nice long gun, too," the man said. "Eight-gauge?"

"Yep."

"Makes a big hole," the man said.

"Does," I said.

"You work here?" he said.

"Here and there," I said.

"I'm looking for a fella named Virgil Cole," the man said. "Might you be he?"

"Nope," I said. "Name's Everett Hitch."

"Chauncey Teagarden," he said. "You're with Cole, are you not?"

He didn't offer to shake hands. I didn't, either.

"I am," I said.

"Know where to find him?"

"I do," I said. "Why do you want to see him?"

"Heard so much about him," Teagarden said.

I nodded. We were both quiet.

"Seems to me," I said after a short time, "that I've heard some 'bout you."

"All good, I hope."

"Heard you did gun work," I said.

"Some."

"What brings you to Appaloosa?" I said.

"Just drifting," he said.

"Planning on staying?" I said.

"Don't expect to be here long," Teagarden said.

"Planning on any work while you're here?" Teagarden smiled.

"See if any comes my way," he said. "I'd surely like to meet Virgil Cole."

"Probably sitting in front of the Boston House," I said. "I'll walk up with you."

" 'Preciate it," Teagarden said.

27

We left the Golden Palace and turned up
Main Street. Virgil was sitting where we sat,
in front of the Boston House. He stood as
we came toward him. There was nothing
sudden in the movement. He was seated.
Then he wasn't. I'd never seen Virgil hurry,
except that everything he did, he seemed to
do it before anyone else.

"Virgil Cole?" Teagarden said.

"Yep."

"Chauncey Teagarden."

Virgil nodded. Neither man put his hand
out.

"You was up in Telford," Virgil said.

"Indeed," Teagarden said.

"Osage County War," Virgil said.

Teagarden nodded.

"Pleasure," Teagarden said.

"Likewise," Virgil said.

Since they had come in sight, each had
looked exclusively at the other.

"Not doing law work," Teagarden said.

"Nope."

"You and Hitch keeping order in some saloons," Teagarden said.

"Yep."

Then Teagarden nodded slightly.

"Well, I'm glad I got to meet you," Teagarden said. "The great Virgil Cole."

Virgil didn't comment.

"Maybe see you again," Teagarden said.

"Maybe," Virgil said.

Teagarden turned and walked off down Main Street. Virgil watched him go.

"Says he's just drifting," I said.

"He ain't just drifting," Virgil said.

"Here on business?"

"He's here to kill somebody."

"You now that," I said.

"It's what he does," Virgil said.

"Why'd he want to see you?"

Virgil smiled.

"So he'd know what I looked like," Virgil said.

"You think it's you?" I said.

"I don't think he was just being neighborly," Virgil said.

"Anything personal?" I said.

"Chauncey Teagarden? Hell, no. He got no feelings. Somebody hired him."

"We know who that would be," I said.

"Probably," Virgil said.

"We gonna do anything about it?" I said.

"We'll await developments," Virgil said.

28

I was leaving the Boston House to start my evening rounds when Laurel came full speed through the swinging doors and ran into me. I caught her and held her for a moment as she looked wildly around the room.

"Virgil?" I said.

She nodded. I knew she couldn't talk to me. So with my arms still around her I bellowed back into the saloon for Virgil. When he appeared I let her go, and she pressed herself against him. He put his head down, and she whispered in his ear. Virgil listened to Laurel completely, like he always did.

"Okay," he said. "We'll go out and you can sit with me and Everett while we discuss this."

Laurel nodded. We sat in front of the saloon.

"Laurel says that Allie told Mrs. Callico that Pony and his brother are up in Resolution."

Laurel leaned over and whispered for a long time to Virgil. He nodded gravely as he listened. Then, when she stopped, he spoke to me.

"Laurel says Mrs. Callico's first name is Olivia."

He looked at Laurel. She nodded.

"Says Mrs. Callico told Laurel to call her Aunt Olivia."

I smiled.

"But since Laurel don't talk," Virgil said, "don't make much difference what she calls her."

"True," I said.

"Laurel says she thinks Mrs. Callico is a horse's ass," Virgil went on. "But that Allie thinks she's the queen of England or somebody."

"So, she told her where Pony went, to suck up," I said.

Laurel pulled at Virgil's sleeve, and he leaned down again. She whispered to him. Virgil nodded.

"Allie was bragging about how she can get her way when she wants it," Virgil said. "Told Mrs. Callico that she made us send Pony away."

"You tell her that?" I said to Virgil.

"I did," Virgil said. "Thought she'd like it."

I nodded.

"Keep forgetting that you can't always count on her," he said.

"Easy mistake to make," I said. "Shot Choctaw Brown for you in Brimstone."

"Keep remembering that," Virgil said. "Keep forgetting how we got to be in Brimstone in the first place."

"Have to assume she'll tell Amos," I said.

"And there's a reward on both Pony and Kha-to-nay," Virgil said.

"Figure we should ride up there," I said.

Virgil nodded.

"We'll go on home, and tell Allie we got to go north for a few days," Virgil said to Laurel. "You don't say a word to her 'bout anything you told me."

Laurel nodded. Then she leaned close to Virgil again and whispered.

When she was done, Virgil said, "Don't worry 'bout Pony. Pony can take care of himself pretty good. And we'll go up."

Laurel nodded. She leaned over again. Again Virgil listened carefully.

Then he said, "Nothing going to happen to Pony Flores. I promise."

She whispered again. Virgil nodded.

"You promise, too, Everett?" he said.

"I promise," I said to Laurel.

She looked at Virgil. He nodded. She

looked at me. I nodded. Then she nodded back at both of us. And smiled.

29

"Laurel's so quiet," Virgil said. "Folks forget she's there, and they say things in front of her."

"Think she'll ever talk?" I said to Virgil.

"Talks to me," Virgil said.

"Think she'll ever talk to anybody else?" I said.

"Don't know," Virgil said.

We were riding easy down a low slope. The horses had settled in for the ride, and picked their way comfortably through the prairie grass. It was warm. The sun was at our backs. And we had a ways to go before we got to Resolution.

"Know why she won't talk to anybody but you?" I said.

"No more'n you," Virgil said.

"Had to do with what happened to her," I said. "But Pony and me saved her, too. How come she only talks to you."

"Knows I'm the smart one," Virgil said.

I nodded.

"Probably it," I said. "I wonder if we took her back east. Boston. Philadelphia. Someplace like that. Maybe a doctor could fix her, or a school, something."

"She don't want to go," Virgil said.

"She said so?"

"She did," Virgil said. "I asked her and she said no."

"Maybe she oughta go anyway," I said. "For her own good."

Virgil shook his head.

"Child's sixteen years old," I said. "How she gonna meet a husband? Have children? Live a life? She won't say nothing."

"Allie'll work with her," Virgil said.

I didn't say anything. Ahead of us a sage hen flurried up and canted off with a lot of wing flapping before she resettled maybe a hundred yards from us.

"We both know Allie got her problems," Virgil said after a while.

"We do," I said.

"Allie's had a lot of hard times of her own," Virgil said. "And you and me can't do it."

"No."

"That monthly stuff, and all," Virgil said.

"We can't do it," I said.

"So, we got to let Allie do it," Virgil said.

"She's trying."

"And we got no one better," I said.

"Nope."

"Maybe we can find a way to send Allie back east with her."

Virgil shrugged.

"Ain't gonna make Laurel go," Virgil said.

"Maybe we should."

"Done too much she don't want to do," Virgil said. "She don't want to talk, she don't have to."

"No," I said. "I s'pose that's right."

"Make it our business to see to it she don't have to do what she don't want to," Virgil said.

"Her whole life?"

"Long as is needed," Virgil said.

"Might mean in the end she don't get to do things she does want to," I said.

"I can see to that, too," Virgil said.

"Not so sure you can," I said.

Virgil shrugged.

"Hell," he said. "Talking ain't worth so much, anyway."

30

Law in Resolution was still Cato and Rose. Frank Rose was a big, showy guy with a handlebar mustache and two pearl-handled Colts. Cato Tillson was small with droopy eyes and a sharp nose. He carried one Colt, with a dark walnut handle. They were both good with Colts. Cato maybe a little better.

"Fella we know got a small place outside of town," Rose said. "Your Indians are sleeping in his hayloft."

"Ain't mine," Virgil said. "And Pony's a breed."

"Well, they ain't give us no trouble," Rose said.

We were in the Blackfoot Saloon, sitting at a round table in the rear, sipping whiskey. Whatever the conversation, as they sat together, Virgil and Cato Tillson always eyed each other. No hostility, just a kind of professional carefulness.

"Anybody else know that?" Virgil said.

"Sure," Rose said. "You used to be here. Town's still 'bout the size of a corncrib."

"There's a bounty on them," I said.

"Didn't know that," Rose said. "You know that, Cato?"

"Nope."

"Make a difference?" Virgil said.

Rose looked at Cato. Cato shrugged.

"Not to us," Rose said. "Might to some folks."

"Police chief in Appaloosa probably knows, by now, that they're here," I said.

"He gonna come after them?"

"Probably will," Virgil said.

"He's the law in Appaloosa," Rose said.

Virgil said, "Yep."

"We the law here," Cato said.

Virgil nodded.

"Bounty hunters out?" Rose said.

Virgil nodded again.

"Might be some Pinkertons, too," he said.

"Might have to hire us couple of deputies," Rose said. "Fellas with experience, say, like you boys."

"Could arrest them," Cato said.

"Cole's Indian?" Rose said.

"Can't make us give up our prisoners," Cato said.

" 'Course they can't," Rose said.

Virgil shook his head.

"Indian won't go for it," he said.

"The breed's brother?" Rose said.

Virgil nodded.

"He won't go to jail," Rose said.

Virgil shook his head.

"We leave the cell unlocked," Cato said.

"He won't," Virgil said.

"Don't make no sense," Rose said. "You think Virgil's right, Everett?"

"Might be," I said. "Often is."

"Well," Rose said. "Let's go talk to them. They don't want to come in, least we can give them a running start."

"Maybe they don't want to run," Virgil said.

Rose looked at Cato again, and leaned back a little in his chair and smiled.

"They want to stay and fight," Rose said. "The least we can do is offer them some high-priced backup."

31

Virgil had brought some whiskey in his saddlebags, and we sat on a plank bench outside of the small barn and passed the bottle. Kah-to-nay declined to drink. A few dark red chickens scratched in the barnyard. A sow with a litter wallowed in a pen beside the barn. Two big-footed farm horses stood placidly in a corral, their heads hanging over the top rail. Our own horses were gathered at the watering trough.

"How long you think before Callico come here?" Pony said.

"Dunno," Virgil said. "All I'm sure is that his wife knows you're here."

"Chiquita warned you," Pony said.

"Yes."

Pony smiled.

"Chiquita doesn't want anything to happen to Pony Flores," he said.

"True," Virgil said.

Pony said something in Apache to Kah-to-nay. Kah-to-nay made a faint shrug.

"If wife don't gossip to him," Pony said. "He maybe not come for weeks."

"Maybe," Virgil said. "Or maybe he's waiting for us at the jail when we get back to town."

"We can arrest you," Rose said. "Put you in the jail. We wouldn't lock the cell. That way, we can say you our prisoner and we won't release you to him."

Kah-to-nay shook his head sharply and spoke in Apache. Pony nodded and held his hand up at his brother.

"How many people Callico bring?" Pony said.

"Gotta leave some people to watch the town," Virgil said. "Figure six or eight, plus himself."

"He any good?" Pony said.

"Amos Callico?" Cato said. "Very good."

Pony nodded.

"You are very good?" Pony said.

"Yes," Cato said.

Pony nodded.

"You and Everett stay, too, Virgil?"

"Long as we need to," Virgil said.

Kah-to-nay spoke again in Apache. Pony nodded.

"So, we all stay here maybe one, maybe two, three weeks, wait for Callico to come arrest me and Kah-to-nay. Maybe big fight."

"Pretty much," Rose said.

Pony nodded.

"Kah-to-nay not go to white jail," Pony said.

All of us nodded.

"Better we go away," Pony said.

"Where?" Virgil said.

"Apache places," Pony said.

"That's where they'll be looking for you," I said.

Pony smiled.

"Some Apache places white-eyes don't go," he said.

"Might depend a little on the white-eye," Virgil said.

Pony grinned wider.

"Yes, Virgil, you go, maybe Everett go with you," he said. "But mostly not."

Virgil nodded.

"You gonna stay on the run all your life?" I said.

"See tomorrow," Pony said. "Don't do Chiricahua good, think about long time from now."

"No," Virgil said. "I'd guess it don't. You need anything."

Pony shook his head.

"You know where me and Everett are," Virgil said.

Pony nodded.

"Speak for Pony to Chiquita," he said.

We all stood up.

"Thank you for help," Pony said to Cato and Rose. "Kah-to-nay know he should say thank you, but he not."

"We know 'bout Kah-to-nay," Rose said.

They shook hands.

Virgil handed the bottle to Pony.

"Take the rest of this with you," he said.

Pony took the bottle. We swung up into our saddles and rode away from them, back toward town.

32

As we came into town, I could see a group of riders gathered at the far end of Main Street in front of the jail, where Cato and Rose kept office.

"Callico," Virgil said.

"Gossip travels fast," Rose said.

"Might be good," Virgil said, "if me 'n Everett drift over and settle in across from the jail."

"Have them between us," Cato said.

Virgil nodded and pulled his horse left. We'd been riding together so long that my horse went with him without prompting. Virgil noticed.

"Smart animal," he said.

"You figure to have trouble with Callico?" I said.

"He ain't gonna be happy," Virgil said, "that Pony and his brother flew the coop."

"True."

Virgil grinned.

"And Frank Rose will annoy him," he said.

"Pretty sure," I said.

"Besides," Virgil said. "Better prepare for what your enemy can do, not what you think he's gonna do."

"True," I said.

"Who was it said that? German fella?"

"Carl von Clausewitz," I said. "Book called *On War.*"

"That's a good one," Virgil said. "Best book you ever give me."

We turned down past the laundry and on past the buildings that lined Main Street. Past the slop barrels, and the privies, the busted wagon wheels and rusting leaf springs, the middens of trash and garbage where coyotes scavenged. We faced Main Street, where the buildings had false fronts. From here you could see that most had been made of green lumber that had split and warped as it dried in the sun. Most towns looked like this from the back side.

"Long way for the police chief of Appaloosa to come chasing a couple of Indians," I said.

"Wants to be the man brought them fearsome savages to justice," Virgil said.

"Like Custer," I said.

Virgil grinned.

"Just like him," he said.

129

We turned up the alley between the Excelsior saloon and the feed store and came out on Main Street in back of Callico, where he and his men sat their horses. Cato and Rose had dismounted and spread out in front of the jail to the width of the building.

Rose was talking.

"Got no idea, Chief, where them Indians went," Rose said.

"How long they been gone?" Callico said.

Rose shook his head slowly. "Hard to say. You know how it is. You notice when you see something. But if you don't see something, you don't notice you're not seeing it."

"For crissake, Marshal," Callico said. "When's the last time you saw them?"

"Week or so, maybe," Rose said. "My work, one day's pretty much like another one. Don't you find it that way?"

"Where were they staying," Callico said. "While they were here?"

"Guess they slept where they could," Rose said. "You know how Indians are."

"One of 'em's an Indian," Callico said. "Other one's a breed."

"Same thing, ain't it?" Rose said. "Got Indian blood, they act like Indians. Never seen it to fail. You?"

Callico shook his head. Short, quick

shakes like he had a fly in his ear.

"You got anything to tell me about the two fugitives?" he said.

"We lay eyes on 'em," Rose said, "we'll arrest them. Ain't that right, Cato?"

"Sure," Cato said.

Callico shook his head again, and wheeled his horse and looked at us.

"You men," he said. "You seen . . . for crissake!"

"Afternoon, Amos," Virgil said.

"What the fuck are you doing up here?" Callico said.

"Visitin'."

"Visiting, my ass," Callico said. "You come up here and warned them fucking fugitives."

"Can't say we did," Virgil said.

"I got a mind to by God take this town apart until I find them," Callico said.

Rose's voice became softer.

"You're the law in Appaloosa, Callico," he said. "Me 'n Cato are the law here. Here you ain't worth lizard scat."

Like Cato and Rose, we were spread out on our side of the street. I had the eight-gauge. Callico looked at us. Then back at Cato and Rose.

"Cato and Rose," Callico said. "I heard of you."

131

"Hell, Chief," Rose said. "Everybody heard of us."

Callico looked back at us.

"Thick as fucking thieves," he said.

I said, "Sorry we can't be more helpful, Amos."

"I can shoot with any of you," Callico said.

"Probably not sitting on a horse," Rose said.

"Probably not," Cato said.

"Come on," Callico said to his men, and headed his horse up Main Street at a gallop.

33

The going underfoot was slow on this stretch as we rode south toward Appaloosa. The horses knew they were going home and didn't need guidance. We gave them their head and, with the reins hanging loose over the saddle horn, let them pick their way through the thorny ground runners and low sage.

"Funny thing," Virgil said. " 'Bout the law."

On a long ride, Virgil, who often went hours without saying anything, was given to musing aloud.

"What's that," I said.

"Up in Resolution," Virgil said. "With Cato and Rose, we was on the side of the law, and Callico was not. When we get back to Appaloosa, Callico'll be the law, and we'll be on the other side of it."

"True."

"But we ain't changed," Virgil said.

"Nope."

"Did the law change?" Virgil said.

"People who decide what it is changed," I said.

"Don't seem right," Virgil said.

"Hell, Virgil, you made the law in every town we marshaled."

"I did," Virgil said. "Didn't I."

"You did," I said. "Will again."

"But it didn't keep changing once I made it," Virgil said.

"No, it didn't," I said. "Still don't. Never does. When we're marshaling you make rules and we call it the law. When we ain't marshaling, you make rules and we call it Virgil Cole."

The horses waded halfway into a small stream and stopped to drink. While they drank, Virgil thought about that.

"And you don't care?" Virgil said.

"Nope. Same rules."

We moved on across the stream and back into the rough scrub.

"And it don't bother you?"

"Hell, Virgil," I said. "You know I don't worry much 'bout such things."

"You let me decide?" Virgil said.

"Generally I agree with you," I said.

"And if you didn't?" Virgil said.

"Depends," I said. "Can't recall you ever

asking me to do something didn't seem like I should."

"But how you know if you should?" Virgil said.

"Most people know what they should do, most of the time," I said. " 'Specially if they ain't married."

"So, why you think I worry about it?" Virgil said.

"Couple things," I said. "You talk about it, but you don't really worry about it. You don't worry 'bout much of anything, 'cept maybe Allie."

Virgil nodded.

"That'd be one thing," Virgil said.

"And you're a good gun hand," I said.

"So are you," Virgil said.

"Yeah, I am," I said. "But you are the best gun hand I ever seen. Maybe the best there is. There's some weight goes with that."

Virgil was looking at some dragonflies hovering over a patch of flowers off to the right.

"Can't just kill somebody 'cause you're quicker'n them," he said.

"No, you can't," I said.

Virgil was quiet for a time as the horses moved carefully along.

"And I don't," he said.

"No," I said. "You don't."

34

Virgil and I were at our post out front of the Boston House when Chauncey Teagarden strolled past us, wearing his ivory-handled Colt.

"Afternoon, Virgil," he said. "Everett."

I nodded.

Virgil said, "Afternoon."

Chauncey stood for a moment looking at Virgil. Virgil had no reaction. Chauncey shook his head slightly.

"The great Virgil Cole," he said.

"You'll be checking that Colt with Fat Willis," Virgil said.

"Of course," Chauncey said.

He looked another moment at Virgil and then went inside.

"You sure do impress him," I said.

Virgil smiled.

"More important I am," Virgil said. "Better he'll feel when he kills me."

"If he kills you," I said.

"If he don't, won't matter to him one way or other," Virgil said.

" 'Cause you'll have killed him."

"Yep."

"It's like he's . . . flirting," I said.

"Is, ain't it," Virgil said.

"Like he wants to get to know you," I said.

"Some fellas like that," Virgil said.

"Enjoy the work more if they know you well," I said. " 'Fore they kill you?"

"Something like that," Virgil said.

"Heard he was from New Orleans," I said. "Won some duels down there."

"Heard that, too," Virgil said.

"Means he got self-control," I said. "Being quick don't make no difference in a duel."

"And he can shoot," Virgil said. "You can't, you don't win many duels."

"So, what we don't know is how fast?" I said.

"Killed Burleigh Ouellette," Virgil said.

"Burleigh was quick," I said. "Chauncey got him?"

"Did," Virgil said.

"And you figure he's here to get you," I said.

"That's what he's here for," Virgil said.

"You figure the general hired him?"

"Be my guess," Virgil said.

137

"So, what's Teagarden waiting for?" I said.

"Needs a situation where it's just me and him. He ain't gonna fight us both at the same time."

I nodded.

"Needs me to draw first, and he's figuring how to do that," Virgil said.

"And maybe he's enjoying the game," I said.

"Probably," Virgil said.

"You think he can do it?" I said.

"Kill me?" Virgil said.

"Yeah."

"No," Virgil said. "I don't."

"You never do," I said.

"Correct," Virgil said.

"And you been right, so far," I said.

35

Laurel, holding her skirt up, came along Main Street at a dead run. When she reached us, she whispered to Virgil. Virgil nodded.

"Pony came to the house," Virgil said to me. "Wants us to meet him west of town at Red Castle Rock."

"I know where that is," I said.

Laurel whispered again to Virgil.

"We won't see him, but if we sit our horses by the rock, he'll find us," Virgil said to me.

"Now?" I said.

Virgil looked at Laurel. She nodded hard.

"Now," Virgil said.

He patted Laurel on the shoulder, and we set out for the livery to get our horses.

We followed the stage road west.

As we rode I said to Virgil, "I noticed something 'bout Laurel today when she come running up to tell us 'bout Pony."

"With her tits bouncing?" Virgil said.

"You noticed it, too," I said.

"Yep."

"She ain't a little girl," I said.

"Nope."

"What are we gonna do 'bout that?" I said.

"Don't know," Virgil said.

The road began to rise gently ahead of us. The horses adjusted to it.

"She know the facts?" I said.

"Hope so," Virgil said.

He grinned.

"Allie sure 'nuff is qualified to tell her 'bout them," he said.

"Virgil," I said. "Laurel don't talk to anybody, 'cept whispering to you."

"I know."

"You can't go round the rest of her life translatin' for her," I said.

"Probably could," Virgil said. "But don't seem like I ought to."

"So, what do we do?" I said.

"Don't know," Virgil said.

"What's Allie say?"

"Allie don't like me talkin' 'bout Laurel to her," Virgil said.

"She don't?"

"Nope. Says I spend too much time thinkin' 'bout Laurel."

"Jesus Christ, Virgil," I said. "She's jealous of Laurel?"

140

" 'Pears so," Virgil said.

"Well, we got to do something about Laurel," I said.

"We do," Virgil said.

"What?" I said.

"Was hoping you'd come up with something," Virgil said.

Ahead of us, with late sun shining from behind it, was the high remnant of ancient red rock that looked a little like the tower of a castle.

We stopped close to its base and sat our horses in its shadow, and pretty soon Pony Flores rode around the base and stopped beside us.

36

"How is Chiquita?" Pony said.

"She's fine," Virgil said.

"She talk yet?" Pony said.

"Just to me," Virgil said.

Pony nodded.

"Kah-to-nay has gone to fight Blue-Eyed Devil," he said.

Virgil nodded.

"Never could abide us," Virgil said.

Pony shook his head.

"Kha-to-nay think you betray him," Pony said.

"You know we didn't," I said.

"I know," Pony said. "Kah-to-nay not know."

"Kha-to-nay fighting white men by himself?" Virgil said.

"No, go back to reservation, get others. Maybe fifteen, they leave reservation, keep moving."

"Raiding?" Virgil said.

"*Sí.*"

"Live off what they take in a raid?"

"*Sí.*"

"So they got to keep raiding."

Pony nodded.

"Where?" Virgil said.

"Come this way," Pony said. "Appaloosa."

"He'd attack the town?" I said.

"Maybe not," Pony said. "Maybe small ranch, maybe homesteader. Maybe posse come out after them; maybe they attack town."

"While the posse's out roaming the plains," I said.

"*Sí.*"

"He ask you to join him?" I said.

"*Sí.*"

"And you didn't," I said.

Pony shook his head.

"How'd he take that?" I said.

"He say I am traitor to Chiricahua people," Pony said. "I say I go with him, I am traitor to myself."

"So, how you want to handle this," Virgil said.

"I cannot kill my brother," Pony said.

Virgil nodded.

"He kill you?" Virgil said.

"No," Pony said.

143

"So, we stop him and don't kill him," Virgil said.

"Cannot go to jail," Pony said.

"Stop him, don't kill him, turn him loose," Virgil said.

"Won't he go right back to it?" I said.

"Maybe will," Pony said.

"What do we do 'bout that?" I said.

"Be Pony's call," Virgil said.

"How bad is the raiding?" I said.

"Burn, torture," Pony said. "Scare white men."

"Don't abide no torture," Virgil said.

The sun had set. But the western sky was still light, and it was still darker in the shadow of the rock than it was on the prairie. We sat silently in our saddles. The horses were cropping the meager grass near the rock.

"You with them for any raids?" Virgil said.

"With them, not raid," Pony said.

"Army after them?" Virgil said.

"Yes, but not close," Pony said.

The horses moved slowly, looking for grass. We let them move. The sky to the west continued to darken very slowly.

After a time Virgil said, "How soon you figure they'll get here?"

"I left them two days ago," Pony said.

Again we were quiet. The only sound was

the movement of the horses as they grazed.

"We can't let them do it," Virgil said.

"What about Kah-to-nay?" I said.

"We do what we can for him," Virgil said. "But we need to stop him."

Neither Pony nor I said anything.

"You okay with that, Pony?" Virgil said.

"*Sí.*"

"You gonna be involved?" Virgil said.

"Spring in hollow near rock," Pony said. "I stay here. See them come, I ride in, tell you."

"You gonna be with us when the balloon goes up?" Virgil said.

"Be with you," Pony said. "Not kill Chiricahua."

"So, what will you do?" I said.

"Maybe keep Chiricahua from kill you," Pony said.

37

"You help these two renegades escape," Callico said. "And now you come asking me to round them up for you?"

"Giving you information," Virgil said.

"Which I take to be bullshit," Callico said. "Who are we fighting here? Alexander the Great?"

"They'll lure the fighters out of town," I said. "And come in behind you, and tear the place up."

"Sure thing," Callico said. "So we stay in here and let them loose on the farms and ranches. Won't that look good."

"Bring the small outfits in," Virgil said. "Big ones, like Laird, can take care of themselves."

"Well, isn't that dandy," Callico said. "I hide here in town with the homesteaders, and let the important landowners fight their own battles."

"For crissake, Callico," I said. "This ain't

about the next election."

"You hadn't gone up to Resolution and warned 'em," Callico said, "wouldn't be having this problem."

Virgil stood.

"Nice talking with you, Amos," he said.

He turned and left, and I went with him.

As we walked up Main Street, Virgil said, "Horse's ass."

"Thinks it's his chance to be a hero of the Indian wars," I said.

"Like Custer," Virgil said.

"Just like that," I said.

"Couple ways this could go," Virgil said.

I nodded.

"They can lure Callico out of town and come in and chew up what he's left behind."

"Or," Virgil said, "they can lure him out and cut him to ribbons like they did to Custer up in Montana."

"Or both," I said.

Virgil stopped and looked at me and thought about it, and nodded.

"Yeah," he said. "I was Kah-to-nay I'd do both. While I had them chasing after me out on the plains I'd come in here and fuck up the town. I'd let a few people escape so they'd run to Callico."

"And when Callico come roaring back into town with blood in his eye, you'd have a spot picked out, and you'd ambush him," I said.

"Both birds with one shot," Virgil said.

"If Kha-to-nay's that smart," I said.

"Don't know 'bout Kah-to-nay," Virgil said. "But Callico's that stupid."

"He is," I said. "So, what do we do?

"We stay in town," Virgil said. "Can't be leaving Allie and Laurel alone."

"Might take more'n you and me," I said.

Virgil grinned.

"Most things don't," he said.

"Two dozen Apache warriors?" I said.

"Might be time to have a talk with General Laird," Virgil said.

"Providing he don't shoot us on sight," I said.

"He's got Chauncey Teagarden for that," Virgil said. "And Chauncey ain't ready yet."

"How do you know he ain't ready?" I said.

"Know boys like Teagarden all my life," Virgil said. "He likes to play with it first."

"And he might want us around to help with the two dozen Apaches," I said.

38

The Lazy L still had the layout it had when it was Randall Bragg's place. But a lot of sprucing had been done since Bragg's rat pack had moved on. We sat in the big front room of the main ranch building while we waited for General Laird, and drank scotch whiskey that a Chinese houseboy poured for us from cut-glass decanters.

"They sell the stuff in them bottles?" Virgil said.

"Nope, sell it in regular bottles," I said. "Those are decanters."

"Don't look like they'd travel good," Virgil said.

"No," I said. "They don't."

General Laird came in through a side door. Teagarden was with him. Chauncey wasn't wearing a hat indoors. He had on a ruffled white shirt and a black silk vest. The ivory handle of his Colt gleamed on his hip. Virgil and I both got to our feet.

"Enjoy my whiskey?" the general said.

"Surprised you offered it," Virgil said.

"No man comes to my home without the offer of a drink," the general said. "Even you."

A little off to the general's right, and a step behind him, Chauncey smiled at us.

"Virgil," he said. "Everett."

We both nodded.

On the wall over the big fireplace at one end of the room was a painting of General Laird in full CSA uniform. There were photographs of the general alone and with his troops. On the buffet at the other end of the room was a painting of a good-looking young woman, probably the general's wife when they were young. And beside it, ornately framed, was a recent photograph of Nicky Laird.

"No reason to pretend we're friends," Virgil said. "Got some renegade Apaches jumped the reservation. Coming this way."

"Riders?" the general said.

"Yep."

"How many?"

"Maybe fifteen, twenty," Virgil said. "Maybe a few more."

"Hell," the general said. "We got 'em outgunned on this ranch."

"Ain't gonna fight 'em on this ranch," Vir-

150

gil said. "They gonna chop up some of the small spreads outside Appaloosa."

The general nodded.

"Till they form a posse and go chasin' them," the general said. "And the Apaches swing in behind 'em and hit the town."

"Yep."

"Callico ought to bring in all the folks can't defend themselves," the general said. "And stay in the town."

"Yep."

"He won't," the general said.

"Nope," Virgil said.

"Callico's a horse's ass," the general said.

"I thought he was your man," I said.

"Best I've got," the general said. "How you know all this 'bout the Apaches?"

"Fella told me," Virgil said.

"Ever fight Indians?" the general said.

"Some," Virgil said. "Everett here's fought a lot of them."

"Army?" the general said.

I nodded.

"Everett's been to West Point," Virgil said.

"Went there once myself," the general said, "when it was all the same country."

"Still is," I said.

The general shrugged slightly.

"Never owned a slave," he said. "Don't believe in it. You boys can't explain things

151

to Callico?"

"Wants to be a hero of the Indian wars," Virgil said.

"Against fifteen reservation Apaches," the general said.

"Yep."

"Can't give you none of my boys to protect the town," the general said. "They gotta protect the ranch."

"Know that," Virgil said. "But I figured you could give me Chauncey."

The general stared at Virgil for a considerable period. Then he looked at Chauncey.

"Sure," Chauncey said. "I can give you a hand."

39

Virgil and I were sipping corn whiskey on Virgil's veranda when we looked up and Pony was there, soundlessly sitting his horse in the shadows.

"They are here," he said.

"Where?" Virgil said.

"Hills, south, near water falling," Pony said.

Virgil glanced at me.

"Squaw Falls," I said. "Couple hours' ride."

"Who's out that way?" Virgil said.

"Compton McCaslin, works the place with his two sons," I said.

"Any hands?" Virgil said.

"Nope."

"Women?"

"Wife of one of the sons," I said.

"They will kill men," Pony said. "Burn ranch. Rape woman, and send her into town."

Pony looked up at the moon in the black sky.

"Probably happen by now," he said.

"Maybe Callico can send some people out to bring the other settlers in," Virgil said.

"Kah-to-nay like that," Pony said.

"Because it will split up the white-eye force," Virgil said.

"Pick off some, make more come," Pony said. "Good both ways."

"You think he's watching the town?" I said.

"Yes."

"He know you're here?" Virgil said.

"No."

"You're sure?" I said.

Pony looked at me.

"You're sure," I said.

I looked at Virgil.

"Can't save everybody," I said.

"You can't," he said. "Pony, you staying."

"I stay," Pony said.

"How you want to play it with your brother?" Virgil said.

"Get him away, before he killed," Pony said.

"How you want us to play it?" Virgil said.

"Same, if you can. If you can't, you have to do what you do."

"Everett," Virgil said. "Time for you to

154

ride on up to General Laird's and collect Chauncey Teagarden. Tell the general he might want to put some pickets out, too."

40

They found the woman lying naked in the south stage road. She had been badly beaten, but she was alive, the blood drying dark on her pale body. The shotgun messenger put his coat around her and held her half across his lap while the driver pushed the tired team hard into Appaloosa.

Virgil and I watched from in front of the Boston House as they took her up the outside stairs to Dr. Peloquin's office above the Café Paris. A crowd gathered outside. Callico showed up promptly, pushed through the crowd, up the stairs, and into Peloquin's office. The saloons began to empty out. The crowd got bigger.

With his hat tilted down over his forehead and his arms folded across his chest, Virgil leaned against one of the roof's support posts.

"Here we go," he said.

"Callico got down there quick," I said.

"Would you wager against him making a speech from the top step when he comes out?" Virgil said.

"No bet," I said.

Chauncey Teagarden came out of the Boston House wearing a black bowler hat, a pink-striped white shirt, and a black string tie. He was carrying a big cup of coffee.

"Amos won't have much trouble working 'em up," Teagarden said. "Half of them are drunk already."

"Tend to be out front," Virgil said. "While the booze is working."

Teagarden grinned.

"Tell who's sobering up the quickest," he said. "By who's dropping back the fastest."

"If they're lucky," Virgil said. "Otherwise they the first ones killed when the balloon goes up."

"Virgil," Teagarden said. "You and me've made a good living shooting fellas like that."

"When I had to," Virgil said.

"Why else," Teagarden said. "Ain't much glory in it."

"Here he comes," Virgil said.

Callico stepped out of Peloquin's office and looked down at the crowd from the top step. He waited. Someone shouted, "We're with you, Amos." Someone else shouted, "Kill the heathen bastards." Callico waited.

Teagarden looked at us and grinned.

"You notice nobody has shouted, 'How's the woman?' " he said.

"They don't care," Virgil said.

"Nope," Teagarden said. "They don't. She's served her purpose."

From the crowd in front of Callico, someone started to chant, "Posse, posse."

Others took it up. Callico waited a little longer as the chant built. Then he put a hand up like he was going to turn stones into loaves of bread. The crowd quieted.

"Dr. Peloquin," he said, "tells me she won't die."

The crowd cheered. Callico waited for them to quiet.

"Though surely she must have wished to die, these last hours. Her husband is dead. Her father-in-law, her brother-in-law. All murdered by the red niggers," Callico said. "She herself abused in extent and manner I cannot speak of in a public forum."

The crowd's sound was indecipherable. It was now simply massive communal noise. Callico let it subside.

"I have been warned," Callico said, "that to pursue these heathen beasts is to put the town at risk."

The crowd was suddenly silent. Something real was about to be discussed.

"Are we men?" Callico said softly.

The crowd listened. I could almost feel it lean forward.

"Are we white Christian men?" Callico roared.

The crowd screamed that we were.

"Is there a man among us who will not join us?" Callico shouted.

The crowd screamed that, no, there were no men who would not join him.

"Even the great Virgil Cole," Callico said. "I can see him from here, in front of the Boston House."

He raised his voice as if he had to make himself heard that far away.

"Will you be joining us, Virgil?"

Virgil stood as he had during the entire performance, hat down, arms folded. He gave no sign that he had heard Callico.

"Of course he will," Callico said. "And his friends."

The mob cheered.

"I'll have my full police force armed and ready for the field," Callico said. "Right here, in the street, mounted and ready to ride, in one hour. I want every man jack of you that owns a gun to join us here with it and lots of bullets, ready to ride."

The mob made its guttural scream. Callico came down the stairs and pushed

159

through the idolatrous crowd toward the police station. Some of the crowd followed him a ways and then began to break up and go home to get ready.

Chauncey Teagarden watched them move away.

"Be like bossing a fucking cattle drive," he said.

"It will," I said.

"He won't get within ten miles of the Indians."

" 'Less they let him," I said.

"In which case they massacre his posse," Teagarden said. "Half of them haven't shot anything bigger than a jackrabbit in their life. They'll probably be drunk. If he does catch them, what's he gonna do, trample 'em to death?"

"He knows all that," Virgil said.

"And he's gonna do it anyway?"

"Ain't about the Indians," Virgil said. "Or the posse. Or the dead men. Or the woman got hurt."

"He wants to be president of the United States of America," I said.

"It's about Callico," Virgil said.

41

We sat our horses with Pony Flores behind Red Castle Rock. Chauncey Teagarden was with us. Pony raised his hand and then put his finger on his lips. The horses stood quietly. There was no wind. We listened.

Then Virgil said, "Callico."

Pony nodded. The sound was very faint. A low murmur of hoofbeats. Virgil scanned the horizon.

Then he said, "From the northeast."

And there it was, a faint drift of dust, kicked up by the faint beat of hooves.

"Kah-to-nay leave big trail toward river," Pony said. "Over there."

We looked west, where, in the distance, the river ran straight north to south in the deep trench it had dug itself.

"Square Stone River," I said. "Hard river to get across. Deep, ten-foot banks straight up and down."

"Kah-to-nay lead them to ford," Pony said.

"And across?" Virgil said.

"*Sí.*"

Virgil nodded to himself. There were things Virgil didn't get. But none of them had to do with his profession. And the things he did get, he got right away.

"Everett," Virgil said. "You done a lotta Indian fighting when you was soldierin'."

"I did."

"You know the ford?"

"I do," I said.

"How many men would it take to hold the ford?" Virgil said.

Pony smiled. I thought about the ford for a bit.

Then I said, "Depends how bad the enemy wants to cross, but probably 'bout four with Winchesters."

"So," Virgil said. "Kah-to-nay makes it look like he and his men crossed. Which they didn't. Callico goes hell for leather across the ford, 'cause he don't want to get caught in the water. Kah-to-nay puts, say, four riflemen in the rocks to hold the ford and takes the rest of his bucks hell-bent for Appaloosa. Where the only gun in town is the derringer Pony gave Laurel."

Teagarden looked at Pony.

"That right?" he said.

Pony smiled.

"*Sí,*" he said.

"Smart Indian," Teagarden said.

"Younger brother," Pony said.

"That how he learned stuff like this?" Teagarden said.

"*Sí,*" Pony said.

"He tell you he was gonna do this?" Teagarden said.

"No," Pony said.

"But you know," Teagarden said.

"*Sí.*"

"Because that's what you'd do," he said.

Pony nodded.

"What I would do," Pony said.

Teagarden looked silently at Pony for a moment.

"Me, too," he said.

We sat and watched the barely discernible dust cloud move ahead of the barely audible sound of the horses.

Then I said, "Time to head back to Appaloosa?"

"I believe it is," Virgil said, and turned his horse northeast.

163

42

We put Allie and Laurel in the Boston House, on the second floor in front.

"Lock the door, stay inside," Virgil said, "until me or Everett tells you to come out."

"Do you think they'll come soon?" Allie said.

"Yes," Virgil said. "You got a gun?"

"Yes."

"Laurel, too," Virgil said.

"The one Pony gave her. She always has it," Allie said.

Laurel took the derringer out of her skirt pocket and showed it to Virgil. He nodded. She stepped close to him and whispered. Teagarden and I stood at the front windows, looking down.

"Pony's on watch," Virgil said.

Laurel nodded. Her face was pale and very tight. She swallowed hard. And her movements were stiff.

"Ain't gonna let them near you," Virgil said.

Laurel nodded stiffly.

"Somehow they get in here," Virgil said quietly to Allie, "you know what to do."

Allie nodded.

"How many will come?" she said.

"Pony says between fifteen and twenty."

"And there's only four of you," Allie said.

"More like three and a half," Virgil said. "Pony said he won't shoot no Indians."

"How can you stop them?" Allie said.

Virgil smiled faintly.

"We shoot very good," he said.

He was wearing his Colt, and a second one stuck in his belt. He carried a Winchester and two bandoliers of .45 ammo. The ammo fit the Winchester and both Colts. I had two Colts and the eight-gauge, and ammo. Chauncey wore a two-holster gun belt with matching ivory-handled Colts. There were bullets in the loops on the gun belt. He had a Winchester, too, and extra ammo in a pigskin satchel.

"Pony's coming," I said.

"How fast?"

"Easy trot," I said.

Virgil nodded toward the door, and Teagarden and I started out.

"We'll be back for you," Virgil said to the women.

Allie looked nearly as pale as Laurel did.

"Can't you stay with us?"

"Don't want to draw fire or attention," Virgil said. "We'll be back."

"I pray that you are," she said.

Laurel stood stone still and watched us as we started out the door.

"Lock it behind us," Virgil said.

"Come back for us," Allie said.

Her voice sounded scratchy.

"Always have," Virgil said.

43

We were standing in the empty street when Pony arrived. Most of the town still believed that Callico's heroic posse would banish the red heathen. But they were staying inside anyway.

"Maybe forty minutes," Pony said as he slid off his horse. "Kha-to-nay, and eighteen warrior."

Virgil nodded.

"Callico on the other side of the river?"

Pony nodded.

"Three warrior with Winchesters on this side," Pony said.

"Only way to get across would be to put the whole posse into the ford at once," I said.

"Lose half of them," Chauncey said. "If you do."

"Callico won't have much luck getting them to take that kind of casualties," I said.

" 'Specially now that they ain't drunk,"

Chauncey said.

Virgil was looking at the street.

"Where they gonna come in?" he said to Pony.

"Kah-to-nay ride straight in down Main Street. Make him feel good. He think no guns here."

"Damn near right," Virgil said. "You sure 'bout this?"

"What Pony would do," he said.

Virgil nodded.

"Everett, take that fucking siege gun up onto the second-floor balcony above the bank," he said.

"Teagarden," Virgil said. "In the hayloft over the livery stable. Try to seem like several people."

"I always seem like several people," Teagarden said.

"You gonna fight?" Virgil said to Pony.

"Not kill Chiricahua," Pony said. "Where Chiquita?"

"In the Boston House," Virgil said. "Upstairs front. With Allie."

Pony nodded.

"Not draw attention," he said.

Virgil nodded.

"You and me," he said. "Front of the pool room across the street. Behind the water trough."

He looked at all of us.

"Let them come in. I'll stop them here, between Everett and Teagarden. Wait for me to shoot."

Teagarden and I both nodded and headed off for where Virgil had told us to be. Chauncey Teagarden had probably been brought to town to kill Virgil Cole. And might still be planning to try. But right now he obeyed Virgil's orders without question, just like everybody always did.

I set up behind the railing of the upstairs porch, made sure all the weapons were loaded, laid a bandolier of ammunition out on the floor, and waited.

44

They came single-file straight down Main Street, with space between them so that each target was single. Kha-to-nay was first. There were vertical white lines painted beside each eye, and his chin was painted black. He was bare-chested, riding a tall bay horse marked with similar war paint. There was a big bowie knife on his belt and a Winchester resting across his saddle in front of him. I could almost hear the collective gasp of the old people, women, and children peering out of their civilized houses at these other people.

He looked carefully left and right as he came. It was probably the way Caesar had looked, riding into a conquered city. He saw me, and pointed at me. They kept coming. I counted them as they came. Ten men, plus Kah-to-nay. Either Pony was mistaken or there were eight missing. Pony was rarely mistaken. When the column was halfway past me, Virgil stepped out from the pool room and walked slowly to the middle of the street. He would have seen the number. He would know there were eight fighters missing.

"Virgil Cole," Kah-to-nay said. "Why are you not out across the river with the other fools?"

His English was flawless, except that it was too precise, like something carefully learned.

"Speaking English now," Virgil said.

"I am here to burn your town to the ground," he said. "I will take some women, probably, and kill everyone else. Therefore it is appropriate to speak the language of the Blue-Eyed Devil."

"But first you want to brag about it," Virgil said.

Again Kah-to-nay shook his head sharply.

"My brother who calls himself Pony Flores says you are his friend. My brother is no longer Chiricahua, but he is my brother. You may ride away, before we begin."

I was shocked. *"You may ride away"? Virgil Cole?*

"Pony is my friend," Virgil said. "And because you are his brother I will make you the same offer."

Kah-to-nay stared at Virgil for a time.

"I will try not to kill you," Kah-to-nay said.

"And me you," Virgil said.

"But if I must," Kah-to-nay said, "I hope you find that it is a good day to die."

"I s'pect they're all about the same," Virgil said.

Without raising his voice, and looking straight at Kah-to-nay, Virgil said, "Anybody see the other eight Indians?"

"Four of them." Chauncey Teagarden's voice came from the stable. "Livery corral behind me. One street over."

"Other four are probably one street over the other way," Virgil mused.

Kah-to-nay turned his head and spoke to his warriors in Apache. Then silence.

Kah-to-nay looked back up at where I was, and over at where Teagarden was.

"How many are you?" he said.

"Enough," Virgil said.

Kah-to-nay raised his voice slightly and said something in Apache. From the pool room, Pony answered.

Then Kah-to-nay began to back his horse slowly away from Virgil. Suddenly he put his head back and screamed. It was a shocking sound in the twisting silence, a sound from another world. He kicked his horse forward and drove him straight at Virgil.

172

Just before he reached him he yanked the horse right and drove the horse down the alley past the Boston House. His warriors came behind him, running straight at Virgil and turning just as they reached him, half going left. Half going right. Virgil stood motionless as they ran at him.

As soon as the Indians disappeared down the side street, a wisp of smoke began to rise on the left, from behind the buildings facing Main Street. Then smoke came from the right. I could smell the coal oil.

In the center of the empty street Virgil put his hands above his head and gestured for us to join him. The balloon was up.

45

The flames were beginning to frolic above the rooflines. The smoke was thick and black and smelled of coal oil. No Indians were in sight on Main Street. But there were periodic gunshots from the side streets, and people, mostly women and children, rushed out of them and began to mill on Main Street.

"He's corralling them on Main Street," I said.

"Then kill them," Pony said.

"Can't fight the fire," Virgil said. "Can't protect all the people. Only thing we can do is kill Apaches. Too few of us to spread out. We stay together. Kill any Indian we see."

He looked at Pony.

"Have to," he said.

Pony nodded.

"Boston House not burning yet," he said.

"It will," Virgil said.

"I go there," Pony said.

Someone released two horses from the livery, and they skittered together down Slate Street and toward the open prairie.

"Indians gonna collect them later," Chauncey said.

"And a lotta scalps," I said.

We moved in the same direction down Bow Street. At the end of the block where Bow crossed Sixth Street two Apaches with Winchesters held their excited horses hard as they stepped and turned, blocking the street. Virgil killed them both.

"Roof," Chauncey said, and killed an Apache straddling the ridgepole. The Indian tumbled off the ridge and rolled down the roof slant and fell to the street. His Winchester stayed halfway down the roof. Next door a building collapsed, the roof falling in with an explosion of flame, and smoke, and sparks, and debris.

A brave came out of an alley in front of us and rode straight at us, firing a big old Navy Colt. Indians in general were not great shooters, and the fact that we were standing, and they were shooting from horseback, gave us another edge. The tight choke of eight-gauge shot hit the Indian full in the chest and knocked him backward off his horse as if he had run into a wall. Somewhere a woman screamed. We could hear a baby crying above the roar of the flames. And occasionally came the awful scream of a war cry. We moved up Sixth Street to Slate and turned the corner. Virgil and I stayed tight to the wall. Chauncey Teagarden had an ivory-handled Colt in each hand.

"Fuck this," he said, and stepped into the center of Slate Street, heading back toward Main. A bullet kicked up dirt in front of him and, almost negligently, he snapped off a shot with his left-hand gun and killed an Indian on a pinto horse. Main Street was full of terrified citizens milling desperately in the searing heat, under a pall of black smoke. The Indians herded them the way cowboys herded cattle. Mounted and moving among the citizens, the Apache were not easy targets. Teagarden stayed in the open street. Gunfire continued to miss him. If we got out of this we'd learn a couple of things. Teagarden could shoot. And he didn't scare easily.

Suddenly the shooting stopped. The flames still tossed and snarled above the buildings, and the smoke still hung low over the street. But it seemed somehow as if everything stopped when Kha-to-nay rode into the maelstrom with four warriors behind him. A young girl with her skirts pushed up high on her bare legs straddled

176

the big bay horse in front of Kha-to-nay, clamped against him by Kha-to-nay's arm holding the reins. It was Laurel. With his left hand Kha-to-nay pressed the edge of a bowie knife against her stomach.

"Virgil Cole," Kha-to-nay bellowed. "Put down your guns and show yourselves, or I will gut your little whore right here."

Virgil stood in the doorway of the hardware store, looking at the situation. We could not let Laurel be cut. We could not give up our guns.

Pony Flores appeared from behind the Boston House, riding a horse with no saddle. Kha-to-nay raised a "hold your fire" hand to his troops, as Pony's horse picked his way through the terrified crowd. He stopped beside Kha-to-nay. On Kha-to-nay's left side. Laurel stared at him.

"Chiquita," he said to her. "I have come get you, again."

Kha-to-nay spoke to Pony in Apache. Pony answered. Kha-to-nay shook his head. Pony spoke again. Kha-to-nay spoke again, louder, shaking his head as he did so. Pony moved so quickly it was hard to follow. He took hold of Kha-to-nay's knife hand and pulled it away from Laurel. His right leg swung over his horse's withers and he was on Kha-to-nay's horse, behind him. The knife appeared from the top of his moccasin. He cut Kha-to-nay's throat, shoved him off the horse, slid forward behind Laurel, got hold of the reins with his arms around her, and kicked the horse forward. As the horse moved we opened up on the four warriors with Kha-to-nay. Three of them went down. Pony flattened Laurel out over the horse's neck and himself over her, and they galloped into the coming darkness of the prairie.

The remaining rider stepped off his horse and squatted next to Kha-to-nay. Chauncey Teagarden raised one of his Colts.

"No," Virgil said.

Chauncey shrugged and held the gun half raised. The Indian began to chant something. In a short while the rest of the still-surviving Indians moved slowly through the crowd and gathered around Kha-to-nay's body. They joined the chant. It was nightfall, and the mourning Apaches gathered around their fallen leader were lit only by the violent flames of the burning town.

"It's over," Virgil said. "You know enough Apache to tell them that?"

"Maybe," I said.

"Say they can take him and go. We won't bother them," Virgil said.

"We got 'em in front of us," Teagarden

said. "We could clean them up for good."

"I know," Virgil said.

He nodded toward the group of Apaches.

"Talk to 'em," Virgil said.

It was as much sign language as me speaking Apache, but I was able to get it across that they were free to take Kha-to-nay and go. The terrified and now delirious crowd in the streets watched them as they rode past bodies they'd killed, out of Appaloosa and away from it. I thought about how far they would have to ride before the burning town would no longer be visible.

"I thought Pony was trying to save his brother," Chauncey said.

"He was," Virgil said.

"Guess he wanted to save the girl more," Chauncey said.

"Guess he did," Virgil said.

46

Virgil and Allie and I were sitting on what was left of the front porch of the Boston House. Much of the town was burned out. Against the charred backdrop of it, women and children and old men were walking aimlessly about.

"Why do you suppose they didn't burn our house?" Allie said.

Virgil shrugged. He was looking down Main Street at some riders coming in. It was Callico.

"Because we're friends of Pony?" I said.

"But he took Laurel and was going to kill her," Allie said.

"Things weren't going the way he wanted," Virgil said.

"And he'd change like that?" Allie said.

"Folks do," Virgil said.

"Savages do," Allie said.

Virgil nodded.

"How'd he get hold of Laurel?" Virgil said.

"She saw the flames. She became hysterical. I tried to keep her with me. But despite all I've done for her, she paid me no mind. She was in the street and he saw her and must have recognized her."

Virgil nodded.

"Got him killed," he said.

"His own brother," Allie said.

"Laurel," Virgil said.

We sat quietly as Amos Callico and his troops straggled back into the smoldering town.

When he saw us, Callico pulled his horse over and stopped. He was spattered with mud, and his clothes were rumpled. He took his hat off.

"Miss Allie," he said, and bowed his head slightly.

"Welcome home, Mr. Callico," Allie said.

"Thank you very kindly, Miss Allie," Callico said.

He looked at Virgil and me.

"Well," Callico said. "We did it."

"We surely did," Virgil said.

"Don't expect those red niggers will try this town again."

"Probably not," Virgil said.

"Thanks for your help," Callico said.

Virgil and I both nodded.

"Well," Callico said, and looked around at

the ruin of a town. "Get me a bath and a night's sleep, and we'll start putting this town back together."

"Gonna cost some money," I said.

"Those Indians are from a United States government reservation," Callico said. "I figure the government owes us."

"Think you can convince them?" I said.

"You boys just watch me," Callico said.

"We will," Virgil said.

Callico turned his horse and fell back in among the returning straggle.

We watched him ride away.

"The hero of Appaloosa," I said.

"He gets government money to rebuild this place," Virgil said, "he will be."

"And they'll never remember what he was doing while the place was burning," I said.

"He knows many important people," Allie said. "I'll bet he can do it."

Virgil nodded.

"When will Pony bring Laurel back?" Allie said.

"Soon as he thinks she's safe," Virgil said.

"Do you know where he took her?" Allie said.

"Red Castle Rock, probably," Virgil said.

"You know where that is?" Allie said.

"I do," Virgil said.

"Well, why on earth don't you go out

there," Allie said. "And bring her back."

"He'll bring her back," Virgil said. "When it's time."

"She's alone, sleeping God knows where with a half-breed tracker," Allie said. "She's sixteen, for God's sake. I'm trying to bring her up right."

"Doin' a fine job," Virgil said.

"And one thing I know," Allie said. "If I know anything, I know men."

Virgil nodded.

"And let me tell you right now," Allie said, "that no good will come of him running off with her someplace alone."

Staring down the smoke-soiled main street of Appaloosa, Virgil turned his head and squinted at Allie.

"I love you, Allie," Virgil said. "Not exactly sure why sometimes. And it looks like I'm keep doing it."

"Why, thank you, Virgil," Allie said.

"But you say some of the goddamned stupidest things I have ever heard," he said.

"Everett," Allie said. "Are you going to let him speak that way to me?"

"Pony killed his brother to save Laurel," I said.

"Does that make him a good candidate for husband?" Allie said.

"Might mean he loves her," I said.

"Oh, piffle," Allie said. "Why does anybody love anybody?"

Virgil squinted at her some more.

"Damned if I know," he said.

47

Fat Willis McDonough, who had no bar to tend at the moment, walked down to Virgil's house from the remains of the Boston House.

"Your friend Pony Flores is in some trouble up on Main Street," Willis said.

"Girl with him?" Virgil said.

"Yep."

Virgil stood.

"You fellas go ahead," Fat Willis said. "Never much liked hurrying."

"Not generally much need," Virgil said.

We started up First Street. And when we reached Main, we turned left.

Pony was there, still mounted, with Laurel sitting behind him, her arms around his waist. Standing in front of them in a semicircle in the street were Callico and his four surviving cops.

"Managed to get two of them killed at the ford the other day," Virgil said.

Standing on the street beside Pony, near his left stirrup, with his two ivory-handled Colts gleaming in the sunlight, was Chauncey Teagarden.

"Fellas want to arrest the hero of the great Apache war," Teagarden said to us. "Don't seem right to me."

We paused so that Callico had Teagarden and Pony in front of him, and me and Virgil behind him. His uniformed officers may have lost some of their confidence in him at the river crossing. They looked at us a little uneasily.

"You are interfering with an officer in performance of his legal duties," Callico said sternly.

Teagarden smiled.

"You bet your ass," he said.

"We are five armed men," Callico said.

"And we're only four," Teagarden said. "What a shame."

Virgil said, "What you arresting him for, Amos?"

"I want to know what part he played in all of this," Callico said. "I mean, his brother was the one burned the town. Why'd this man take that girl? How much did he help his brother with the burning and looting?"

I smiled to myself. They'd been too busy with the burning to do much looting. That would probably have come next day, along with raping, if Pony hadn't cut the whole thing short.

"He helped save your town," Virgil said.

"Got to find that out officially, Virg," Callico said. "Got to take him in."

"No," Virgil said.

"Virg," Callico said. "You gotta understand. We'll turn him loose, soon's we clear him."

Virgil said nothing.

I said, "Callico, we all know that this is about looking like the man in charge at the battle of Appaloosa."

"You're planning to interfere?" Callico said.

"We are," I said.

"All three of you?"

"Four," Pony said.

Callico nodded forcefully.

"We'll discuss this again," he said.

"No," Virgil said. "We won't."

The sound of hammers and saws filled the street. A big freight wagon hulked past, stacked with partially burned lumber, the massive draft horses leaning hard into their harness. Callico turned sharply, jerked his head at his policemen, and walked back down Main Street. We watched them go. Pony looked at Virgil and smiled.

" 'Virg'?" he said.

"My mother didn't even call me that," Virgil said.

"What did she call you?" I said.

"Don't remember," Virgil said.

48

We went back down First Street toward Virgil's house. When we got there, Allie was on the front porch. Laurel slid off the back of Pony's horse and ran to her. Pony stayed on the horse.

"My child is home safe," Allie crooned. "My child is home."

"Don't think she's staying, Allie," Virgil said.

He was standing on the first step of the porch, next to Laurel.

"What," Allie said. "What."

Virgil said, "You stayin', Laurel?"

She shook her head.

"You going away?" Virgil said.

She nodded.

"With who?" Virgil said.

Laurel pointed at Pony.

"You can say his name," Virgil said.

Laurel stared at Virgil.

"You can," Virgil said.

She stared some more. Virgil leaned forward and whispered in her ear. She nodded. He whispered again. She shook her head. He whispered again. She was motionless. Then she looked at Pony. And at me and Allie, and obliquely at Chauncey Teagarden. She looked back at Virgil and then at Pony again.

"Pony," she whispered.

I saw Allie's eyes widen. Her mouth opened. But something stopped her before she spoke.

"You want that, Pony?" Virgil said.

Pony was turned sideways in his saddle. His right foot was in the stirrup, and his left knee hooked over the saddle. He was rolling a cigarette.

"*Sí,*" Pony said, and lit the cigarette.

"Got some money left from Brimstone," Virgil said. "I'll get you some."

Pony shook his head.

"Good way to start, Jefe," he said. "Each other, nothing else."

Virgil nodded.

"Buy her a horse," he said.

Pony smiled.

"I get her horse, Jefe."

Virgil nodded slowly.

"Kinda what I was afraid of," he said.

Pony looked at me and put out his hand.

"Everett," he said.

"Pony."

He looked at Teagarden.

"Gracias," he said.

Teagarden shook his hand.

"On down the road," he said.

Pony nodded. He looked at Allie.

"Señorita," he said.

She was holding her apron up to her face. Virgil stood in front of Laurel with his hands at his sides.

"Wherever you go. Whatever happens. You got some people here who love you."

She nodded. Then put her arms around Virgil and buried her face in his neck and cried. He put his arms around her and stood expressionless, holding her comfortably until she was through.

She stepped away from him and looked at Pony.

"Chiquita," he said, and put out his hand.

She swung up behind him. He turned the horse and kicked him into a trot and they left. All of us watched as they rode off. Allie sniffled loudly.

"Nice ceremony," Teagarden said.

49

Emma Scarlet wore a red wig for business, but since we were more friends than anything else, and since this morning we had finished our business already, she left the wig on its holder while we drank coffee in her room.

"So, the girl ran off with the half-breed," Emma said.

"Laurel," I said. "With Pony Flores."

"Love," Emma said.

"I guess."

We drank some coffee.

"I think Allie was a little upset," I said.

"You do," Emma said.

"Think she was planning on some fine eastern gentleman," I said.

"For crissake, Everett, Laurel didn't even talk."

" 'Cept to Virgil," I said. "And 'fore she left she said Pony's name out loud."

"Golly," Emma said.

"She might have been losing her baby, but she'd only had a baby for a couple years."

"And maybe she didn't mind," Emma said.

"No?" I said.

"Maybe she didn't like the competition," Emma said.

"Competition with who?" I said.

"Laurel," Emma said.

"For?"

"Virgil," Emma said.

"Virgil wouldn't lay a hand on Laurel," I said.

"Don't matter what Virgil would do," Emma said. "It's what Allie fears that matters."

"You think Allie was afraid Virgil would run off with Laurel?" I said.

" 'Course she was," Emma said.

"I don't see that," I said. "I known them since they been together. Virgil never run off on her."

"She ever run out on him?" Emma said.

"She did," I said.

Emma was still naked from our time of business, and as she talked she leaned back and looked at her extended leg.

"Where'd she end up?"

"Pig wallow in Placido," I said. "On the Rio Grande."

193

"How'd she get out of there?"

"Me and Virgil found her, took her out," I said.

"And if you hadn't?"

"She'd a died," I said.

"So, he owes her leavin'," Emma said.

"More than one," I said.

"And if it weren't for him she'd be fucking her life away in some dump down by Mexico."

"So, she'd be worried about anybody," I said.

"Especially a young girl starting to come of age that speaks only to Virgil?"

I nodded and drank some coffee.

"Hadn't thought of it that way," I said.

" 'Course you hadn't," Emma said. "She's a woman." She waved her naked leg around. "You only think of her this way."

"You don't seem to mind," I said.

She shrugged and pointed her toes.

"Not with you," she said.

50

Someone had set up a steam saw at the corner of Main and Second Street, and you could hear it eighteen hours a day, every day, all over town. It was like the base melody for an orchestra of hand tools: hammers, chisels, mallets, and handsaws hovering in lighter cadence. The raucous language of the laborers formed a vocalization.

Several saloons had set up tents with plank-and-barrel bars, and enough people got drunk to keep me and Virgil in business from our headquarters on what was left of the Boston House's front porch.

Virgil was looking at it all.

"We had this many government folks before," Virgil said, "Kah-to-nay wouldn't have attacked."

"And Callico has kissed the ass of every one of them since," I said.

"The hero of the recovery," Virgil said.

"Lot people will remember him for it, and

195

be grateful," I said. "He knows a lot of people. He's brought in lot of money for rebuilding."

"The savior of Appaloosa," Virgil said.

"Been better if he never lost it in the first place," I said.

"Would," Virgil said.

A big lumber wagon pulled by eight oxen drudged up Main Street past us toward the steam saw with a load of logs.

"When they get that cut up," I said, "think they'll cure it proper?"

"Nope."

I smiled.

"Be good not to buy a new building in town for a few years," I said. "Let it dry out."

A handsome two-bench buggy went by in the other direction, pulled by two gray horses. A driver sat on the front seat, and in back was General Laird, with Chauncey Teagarden beside him. Chauncey was wearing a black jacket with conchos, and his ivory handle gleamed in contrast.

"Chauncey's looking good," I said.

"He is good," Virgil said.

"He still here for you, you think?"

"Be my guess," Virgil said.

"Because of the son," I said.

"Yep."

"What are they waiting for?" I said.

"Chauncey likes to play the fish for a rime, 'fore he catches him," Virgil said. "And during the recent Indian thing we was kinda useful."

"I got another theory," I said.

"Figured you would," Virgil said. "Bein' as how you went to West Point and all."

"Things are in a state of some flux," I said.

" 'Flux'?" Virgil said.

"Like flow," I said. "Things are moving and changing."

"Does a river flux?"

"No, it flows," I said.

"Don't it mean the same thing?" Virgil said.

"Pretty much," I said. "Except people just say it the way they say it."

"So, things are fluxing," Virgil said.

I nodded.

"So, Laird may be thinking it's a good idea to have a first-rate gun hand available until things shake out."

"That would be Chauncey," Virgil said.

"And if Chauncey kills you," I said, "he probably would need to go away."

"Not, I'm betting, because of Amos Callico," Virgil said.

"Maybe, maybe not. Depends how things are when he has to decide. But Stringer might come down from the sheriff's office. Hell, I might even get sort of bothersome 'bout it."

"It would make sense for Chauncey to flux on out of Appaloosa after he killed me," Virgil said.

"Which," I said, "would leave Laird without the gun hand that he might need if, say, he finds it too hard to get along with Callico."

"Nicky probably done that work for him before," Virgil said.

"Or wanted to," I said.

Virgil shook his head sadly.

"Wasn't good enough," he said.

"But Chauncey is," I said.

"Maybe," Virgil said.

"And if you kill him . . ." I said.

"Laird's gotta find somebody else."

"Ain't too many in Chauncey's class," I said.

"Nope."

"So, we wait and watch," I said.

"Yep."

"Least he won't back-shoot you," I said. "He'll come at you straight on."

Virgil nodded.

"Be too bad if I have to kill him," Virgil said. "He's been pretty useful so far."

"So have you," I said.

"I have," Virgil said. "Haven't I?"

51

The front of the Golden Palace where it faced the street was still open. And carpenters were bringing in lumber and millwork. But the back of the room was enclosed and there were a few odd tables set up near a bar made from a couple of tailgates.

Buford Posner brought a bottle of whiskey and four glasses to the table where Virgil and I were sitting with Lamar Speck. He poured some whiskey for each of us. Speck raised his glass.

"Almost back," he said, and drank. We joined him.

"Get that front closed in," Speck said. "And you can get started on the finish."

"Got a new bar," Posner said, "coming in from Denver. Amos got them to ship it to me on credit through the Reclamation Commission."

"And got a little finder's fee," Speck said.

"Sure," Posner said. "Amos always gets a

little finder's fee."

"Didn't know we had a Reclamation Commission," I said.

"What Amos calls it," Posner said. "Calls himself commissioner, too."

"He would," I said.

"Not a bad idea, though," Speck said. "Town was originally thrown up building at a time with no oversight. So Amos got together with some of the better-off business interests in town, and he says we got a second chance, let's do it right. And he brings the general aboard, first off, and when people see that, they're interested. Me 'n Buford came aboard."

Virgil seemed interested in the framing work going on in the front of the saloon. But I knew he heard what was being said. Virgil, as far as I know, always heard everything that mattered. And saw everything, and knew what to do.

"How's it work?" I said.

"We all chip in some money, to make a little credit pool, and use it to support loans for people rebuilding. In return they give the commission a say in what they're doing," Speck said.

"Nice position of power," I said.

"Amos put in money," Virgil said.

He was still watching the framers. It was

the kind of thing Virgil liked to watch. Men with a skill practicing it well.

"Mostly the general put up the money at first," Posner said. "Him and Amos is pretty tight. Amos is the commissioner, does most of the legwork."

"You boys get to say much?" I said.

"We have regular meetings," Speck said.

"Truth of the matter," Posner said, "we're in 'cause we can't afford to be out."

I nodded.

"But do you have any say?"

"Not much," Speck said. "Callico and the general are very tight. They pretty much decide everything."

"And it's not just the money," Posner said. "Callico is the law here, and he always has some policemen with him."

"And the general?" Virgil said.

"Teagarden is always beside him," Posner said.

"Any threats?" Virgil said.

"Not direct, but they can back up what they think should happen," Posner said.

"And you boys can't," Virgil said.

"No."

"And you want us to help you."

They said yes at the same time.

Virgil looked at me.

"You want to have the first say, Everett?" he said.

I nodded.

"I don't like it," I said.

Virgil nodded slowly.

"No," he said. "I don't, either."

"We can pay you well," Speck said.

Virgil shook his head.

"Ain't that," he said.

"Are you afraid?" Posner said.

Virgil smiled.

"Long as Everett and me been doing this?" he said. "Nope, we ain't scared."

"You want to end up on the right side of things," Speck said. "When this is all over with and Callico's got the town."

"Everett," Virgil said to me. "Would you explain to these two gentlemen why we ain't gonna do this?"

"What we do," I said to Speck and Posner, "is we kill men. We been doing it for a while and we are better at it than anyone we've come up against so far. Being good at killing men is different than being good at bulldogging a steer or shooting holes in silver dollars. It's serious, and it needs to be done right."

Speck and Posner stared at me and said nothing.

"You're a lawman and right is pretty easy.

You do what the law requires. And you're pretty much sure you're on the right side of things. Until now and then you find that you're not. And you have to kill someone on your own terms."

Virgil nodded. He had always worried about stuff like this more than I did.

"This would be like that," I said. "And we don't want to kill a man on your terms."

"Well," Speck said. "Pretty goddamned fancy for a couple of fucking gunmen."

"Fancy," Virgil said.

52

Virgil and I were having coffee and dried-apricot pie at Café Paris. Through the front window we could see the opening ceremonies for the new Laird bank that the general was opening in Appaloosa.

There was red, white, and blue bunting. There were some speeches. Two guys played banjo. The general was there, of course, in a dark gray suit and some ribbons and an officer's dress sword on a sash. Teagarden was beside him, wearing his ivory-handled Colt. Chauncey was a bear for ceremony.

"Lotta money kicking around Appaloosa these days," I said.

"Callico and the general," Virgil said.

"Yeah," I said. "They've brought in a lot."

"That much money coming and going," Virgil said. "Trouble comes with it."

"Bad element collecting in town?" I said.

"Seems so," Virgil said.

"Anyone special?" I said.

"Well," Virgil said. "There's you and me."

"We cleaned it up the first time, Virgil."

"Might have to again," Virgil said.

"And who'll pay us to do it?"

"Whoever got the most to lose, I expect," Virgil said.

"So, we got some preliminary skirmishes to observe," I said. " 'Fore we know."

Virgil nodded. We both ate some pie, and Virgil drank some coffee. He shook his head.

"Chinaman makes the second-worst coffee in Appaloosa," he said.

"Allie being the worst," I said.

"Yes."

I nodded toward the bank festivities.

"Allie's in attendance," I said.

"I know," Virgil said. "Since Laurel went off, Allie's got a lot of free time."

He drank some more coffee.

"I don't encourage her to spend it cooking," he said.

"I wouldn't," I said.

"She's working her way up in Appaloosa society," he said.

"Which would be, at the moment, Callico," I said. "And the general."

"Callico is through Mrs. Callico," Virgil said.

"The belle of New Orleans," I said.

"Whole damned South," Virgil said.

The Chinaman came out and poured us more coffee. We both drank some and looked across the bright street. Allie was talking to Chauncey Teagarden.

"General's kinda long in the tooth," I said. "But Chauncey ain't."

Virgil nodded and stared across the street at Allie over the top of his coffee cup.

"You and me know Allie, I'd guess," Virgil said, "better'n anybody."

"You know her best," I said.

Virgil shook his head.

"No," Virgil said. "I fucked her and you ain't. But you know her well as I do."

I didn't say anything.

"And she knows that Chauncey is here sooner or later to kill me," Virgil said.

I nodded.

"And she knows that he might succeed."

"Always possible," I said.

"And so you know she's thinking ahead," Virgil said.

I was quiet for a moment, looking across the street. Then I took in some air and blew it out slowly.

"And lining up replacements," I said.

"In case," Virgil said.

"Something happened to you, I'd look out for her," I said.

"She knows that," he said. "She also

knows I go down, you'll probably go, too."

"Probably," I said.

"And even if you don't go down, she knows you won't . . ."

Virgil wobbled his hand a little.

"No," I said. "That's right. I'd look out for her, but I wouldn't, ah, be with her."

"You don't love her," Virgil said.

"No."

Virgil gazed across the street silently.

"I do," he said.

"I know."

"Don't make any sense, does it?" Virgil said.

I exhaled again.

"No," I said. "But maybe it ain't supposed to."

"I want her to feel safe," Virgil said.

"I'll see that she does," I said.

"No," Virgil said. "You can't. 'Cause you won't fuck her and she can't feel safe with no one 'less she's fucking him."

"I know," I said.

"So, let her find somebody to fuck, if I go," Virgil said. "And don't kill him for fucking her."

I nodded again.

"Work out better all around," I said, "you don't die."

"Would," Virgil said. "Wouldn't it."

53

As the town bloomed, the Reclamation Commission bloomed along with it and, in time, was effectively running Appaloosa. Most of the running was done by Laird and Callico, who had come to seem to be almost a single entity. They built a big hall with offices for town government and a big meeting hall on the second floor. They called it Reclamation Hall. Callico moved his offices there from the jail. He and Laird set up offices for the Reclamation Commission there. At the end of a grand mahogany corridor on the first floor, they built a lavish office for the mayor. There was the Reclamation Commission. There was Callico and Laird. The rest of the offices were empty. There was no town government. There was no mayor.

"Bad mistake," Virgil said, walking through the still-virgin offices.

"Building the office first?" I said.

"Longer it sits here," Virgil said, "more pressure to have an election and elect a mayor."

"Which will be either Callico or the general," I said.

"Running against each other," Virgil said.

I nodded slowly without saying anything.

"Ain't ready for that yet," Virgil said.

"Laird might be," I said.

"Maybe he is," Virgil said. "Maybe he ain't. Callico ain't."

"Wants it too bad," I said.

We walked out of the gleaming new office and down the broad corridor.

"Wants everything too bad," Virgil said.

"Wants to be more than he is," I said.

"Not the key to happiness, I'm thinking," Virgil said.

"You'd settle for being what you are," I said to Virgil.

"I have," Virgil said.

"Would you settle for being Callico?" I said.

We opened the heavy front door and went out of the soap-smelling hall and down the stairs. The smell of the town was thick with sawdust and raw wood, horse droppings, and the smell of scorched wood from the steam saw. All drifted across Appaloosa on the easy breeze from the prairie, to which a vestige of sage smell still clung.

"No," Virgil said.

54

The restoration of Appaloosa was complete by the time the fall rains arrived. But the town kept right on building.

On September 1, Amos Callico and General Horatio Laird both announced that they were running for mayor. On September 15, *The Appaloosa Argus* endorsed General Laird.

"Do you think he'd be the best?" Allie said.

"Don't know, don't care," Virgil said. "Hate politics."

"Well, they're what's running," Allie said. "Who you gonna vote for, Everett?"

"Probably Callico," I said.

"Even though the newspaper says it should be General Laird?"

"They probably think he looks like a mayor," I said.

"He was a general, you know," Allie said.

"Part of the problem," I said. "He's used

to working inside a set of rules. And he's used to people doing what he tells them to do."

"I should think that would be good for a mayor," Allie said.

Virgil was standing in the kitchen doorway, looking out at the dark rain soaking into his yard. The sound of it was pleasant. The smell of the new rain was fresh. The mud was probably six inches deep already.

"Not for mayor of a town like Appaloosa," I said. "Never had a mayor before. Never actual like had a government before. Man's gonna get things done in a town like this, hell, most towns, is a liar and a thief. Like Callico. He won't keep his word. He won't honor yours. He doesn't care about you. He doesn't expect you to care about him."

"That's a good mayor?"

"He'll get things done," I said.

"Maybe that's not all he should do," Allie said.

At the open door, Virgil turned and looked for a long moment at Allie.

"By God, Allie," he said. "Maybe it ain't."

55

Business was good in Appaloosa. Virgil and I kept busy buffaloing drunks, and occasionally a little more, in the saloons we serviced. When we weren't busy we spent our time watching the mayoral election unfold in virgin territory.

The rain was meager today. Enough drizzle to keep the streets mucky but not to drive the voters away, and they stood in a damp cluster around the stairs to Reclamation Hall, where General Laird was explaining to them why they would be wise to vote him in as mayor.

"I have led men all my life," he said. "I understand how to run an organization."

"You understand how to run," someone said loudly in the front row.

"I beg your pardon, sir?" Laird said.

"Whyn't you tell 'em how you flat-out run away at Ralesberg," the loud voice said.

"I did no such thing. We won at Rales-berg."

"While you was running, you burned out a refugee camp and slaughtered a bunch of women and children," another voice said just as loudly.

"Sir, that is a lie," Laird said.

He stood very erect in a slightly shabby gray CSA general officer's coat, the light rain drizzling down onto his bare head.

The two voices separated themselves from the front row. One belonged to a tall, raw-boned red-haired man with a weak and unimpressive beard. The other was shorter and thicker, with a dense black beard, wearing a Colt on a gun belt over bib overalls.

"You callin' us liars?" the red-haired man said.

He carried a short-barreled breech-loading cavalry carbine. The people immediately around them moved away.

"Watch Chauncey," Virgil murmured.

Chauncey had been leaning against the frame of the big front door, sheltered from the rain, watching the activity.

"What you are saying, sir, is untrue," Laird said.

"I say you are a back-shooting, barn-burning, gray-bellied coward," the red-haired man said. "Anybody gonna tell me no?"

"I am," Chauncey said.

"Who the hell are you?"

"General Laird is a gentleman," Chauncey said. "He is not a murderous thug. He is not going to descend to a street fight with you."

"And you?" the man with the black beard said.

Chauncey straightened lazily from the door frame and ambled out to stand maybe five feet in front of the two men.

"I am a murderous thug," Chauncey said.

There was silence. Chauncey's ivory-handled Colt, sprinkled slightly with rain-drops, seemed to gleam in the low, gray light.

"If you'd like," Chauncey said, "you get to pick where I shoot you."

"Chauncey," General Laird said. "I appreciate your support. But this is a democratic process. We cannot have people killed."

"I'm not running for anything, General," Chauncey said.

"You are with me," General Laird said.

"Yessir," Chauncey said. "I am."

He smiled at the two hecklers.

" 'Nother reason to vote for General

216

Laird," Chauncey said. "He just saved your lives."

56

Virgil and I were having breakfast in Café Paris when Allie came in with a tall woman in a fancy dress.

"Since you're not willing to eat my cooking in the morning," she said, "I decided to join you."

Virgil and I both stood.

"Please do," Virgil said.

"This is Amelia Callico," Allie said. "Her husband, as you know, is chief of police here. She's been dying to meet you."

We both said we were pleased. Mrs. Callico tipped her head slightly and made the faint hint of a curtsy, and we sat. She looked around.

"How charming," she said.

"Yes, ma'am," Virgil said.

"Do many women come in here?" she said.

"Mostly men," Virgil said.

"We ladies lead such sheltered lives,"

Amelia said. "Unless the men take us, we never go anywhere."

"Lady can't be too careful," I said.

"Virgil and I met here," Allie said. "I was alone and they wouldn't give me biscuits, and he stepped in."

"How gallant," Amelia said, stressing the second syllable.

"Virgil was the marshal here then," Allie said.

"I understand that he was," Amelia said. "And what do you do now for work?"

"Odd jobs," Virgil said.

"For some of the local saloons," I said.

"How nice," she said.

"Covers the cost of breakfast," Virgil said.

"I'm sure," Amelia said.

"That's a beautiful dress, Amelia," Allie said.

"Yes, thank you. I had it made for me in New Orleans."

"You from New Orleans?" Virgil said.

"Yes," she said. "I am. What's good here."

"I'd stick with the biscuits," Virgil said.

"That's all?" Allie said. "Why do you come here when all you eat is biscuits? I can make biscuits for you."

Virgil's face didn't change expression, but something in the set of his shoulders shifted, and I stepped in.

"We eat food that ladies wouldn't like," I said. "Sow belly. Fried pinto beans."

"So, for lady food," Amelia said, "biscuits is what they offer."

" 'Tis," I said.

"Then that's what I'll have," she said.

The Chinaman took our order and went to get it.

"I never understand why they are so silent," Amelia said. "It's as if they hate us."

"Mostly don't speak much English," Virgil said.

"Well, they should," Amelia said. "They're going to come here and live and take our money."

"Sure," Virgil said.

"I wanted to meet you, of course, because of my friendship with Allie," Amelia said. "But also I wanted to suggest an opportunity for you and your friend to make money, and do yourselves some good."

"Open a lady-food café?" Virgil said.

Amelia smiled. She had a very convincing smile.

"Perhaps," she said.

She was a good-looking, full-bodied woman with a mass of reddish-brown hair piled on her head.

"As you know," she said, "my husband, Amos Callico, is running for mayor of Appaloosa. I am convinced that it is only a first step. Indeed, I am utterly convinced that it is the first step on a path that will lead him, ultimately, to become the President of the United States."

I could see that Virgil was trying to look impressed, and I could see that it wasn't working.

"You will certainly make a grand first lady," I said.

"Thank you, kind sir," she said. "I am hoping that you both would wish to join us."

"How would we do that?" Virgil said.

"Help us get the truth out," Amelia said. "There are facts about our opponent that need to be known."

"He ran in combat?" Virgil said. "He slaughtered women and children?"

"Yes, that and more," Amelia said. "There is much in General Laird's past that is shameful."

"And you want us to tell people?"

"The truth must be the basis of any election," she said.

"Beggin' your pardon, ma'am," Virgil said. "But how do we know it's the truth?"

"No pardon needed," she said. "You have my word that anything we tell you is the truth."

"Fellas that fronted up to the general outside Reclamation Hall yesterday?" Virgil said. "They get their information from you."

"Yes, and it is good information. But Laird has a man working for him . . ."

"Chauncey Teagarden," Virgil said.

"Yes. He is quite intimidating."

Virgil nodded.

"From New Orleans, too, you know that?" Virgil said.

"I did not," she said.

"Small world," I said.

Allie smiled at me nervously. No one else paid any attention.

"You figure Teagarden won't intimidate me 'n Everett," Virgil said.

"I'm told that nothing does," Amelia said.

"And if you helped them now, think what it would mean to us," Allie said. "As Mr. Callico moved on up the ladder."

Virgil looked at me. I shook my head. He nodded.

"Nope," he said.

"We will pay you well," Amelia said.

"Nope."

"Why not?" Amelia said.

"Me 'n Everett don't like your husband," Virgil said.

She sat silently for a minute. Then she stood.

"He will be disappointed to hear that," she said, and stalked out of the café.

Allie looked as if she might cry.

57

I had a beer with Chauncey Teagarden in a small saloon called Rabbit's, near the new red-light section of town.

"You're from New Orleans," I said.

"Ah surely am," he said, broadening the accent.

"Did you know that Callico's wife is from New Orleans?"

Chauncey grinned.

"Amelia," he said.

"You do know her," I said.

"Know her," Chauncey said. "She don't know me."

"Tell me 'bout her," I said.

"Queen of Storyville," Chauncey said. "Worked three, four cribs there, 'fore she met Callico and gave up honest labor."

"Ever go to one of her establishments?"

"Hell, when she was first starting out she used to work the bedrooms herself," Chauncey said. "I been to her."

"Callico know that?" I said.

"No, she don't even know that. She was a busy girl when I was going to her. And I didn't shave yet."

"But he knew she was a whore?"

"Oh, sure," Chauncey said. "He went to her, too. Called herself the Countess. That was her trick, always wore a fancy dress. Nothing under it."

"How'd she meet Callico?"

"Don't know," Chauncey said. "Don't know too much about Callico. For a while, I know, he was a trick shooter at a carnival, used to play around New Orleans. Saw him once. Man, could he shoot."

"Clay pigeons?" I said.

"Yep. Fancy ones sometimes. Made of glass."

"Pigeons ever shoot back?"

"Nope."

"Unlikely to," I said.

"God, he was fast, though. And accurate."

"She work the carnival?" I said.

"Doubt it," Teagarden said. "Mighta been a bouncer in one'a her joints and then something clicked and they went off together. 'Cept I heard she took up with a fella by that name, I never thought anything about either one of them until I got here. I recognized her. And when I seen him, I remember him shooting. Ain't all so many fellas named Callico you're gonna run into."

The doors to the saloon were open, and outside the sky was low and dark and there was a sense of something coming. Most people were off the street.

"Something coming," Chauncey said, looking out at the dark street.

"A lot of it," I said.

We carried our beer glasses to the doorway and stood, looking out at the empty street where the wind was beginning to kick a little trash around.

"This thing between Callico and the general is going to turn into something bad," Chauncey said.

"If it does, you're with the general," I said.

"I am," he said.

"You and the general against Callico and his policemen," I said. "He's got a fair number of hands."

"Yeah, but mostly cowhands," Chauncey said.

"You're not a cowhand," I said.

"No," Chauncey said. "I am not."

"So, he needs you to run the tactical command, so to speak."

"I'd say so."

"You didn't come here to fight a war," I said.

"Things change," Chauncey said.

"Forever?" I said.

"Till after the war."

"Then?"

"I do what the general hired me to do, if he still wants it done."

"He don't seem like a man changes his mind much," I said.

"No."

"General's kid required it of Virgil," I said.

"I'm sure he did," Chauncey said. "Virgil Cole don't go around shooting people 'cause he can."

The wind was picking up as we stood, watching in the doorway. It pushed tumbleweed up the street past us. Far to the west, lightning flashed, and in a moment the sound of thunder came to us. No rain yet, but the tension of its pending arrival filled the air.

"Soon," I said.

"I have to go against Virgil," Chauncey said. "I assume that includes you."

"Does," I said.

"Still got that eight-gauge?" Chauncey said.

I smiled.

"Do," I said.

"Won't make it easier," Chauncey said.

"I'll come straight at you," I said. "I don't

227

back-shoot."

"Well, never lost yet," Chauncey said.

"Neither has Virgil," I said.

A single raindrop splattered into the still-dusty street in front of us.

"I know," Chauncey said. "Sorta what makes it worth trying."

58

The rain when it arrived was everything it promised to be. It came down, slanted by the wind, hard and cold and steady. The Callico election rally that had been scheduled for Main Street was moved inside the saloon at the Boston House, with Callico standing on a chair near the bar and half the Appaloosa police department ranged along the outside walls.

"I promise you safe streets in Appaloosa, and open saloons, and more of the same kind of money and development that has been flowing in through my efforts these last months."

Wearing a slicker buttoned to his neck and a confederate cavalry hat pulled down over his eyes, General Laird pushed into the saloon. Chauncey Teagarden came behind wearing a slicker, too. He kept his unbuttoned, holding it closed with his left hand until he got out of the rain. The two men stood in the crowd toward the front of the room.

"My opponent, who, incidentally, has just arrived in the room," Callico said, "will tell you he is qualified to lead because he has been a military man, a commander. Albeit of a rebel power? Don't we then have the right to ask what he commanded his soldiers to do? Would that not tell us what kind of civic leader he might make? Recently some of my supporters spoke publicly of his pusillanimity at Ralesberg. Of his brutality toward woman and innocent children, as he fled the field of battle."

Beside me, Virgil said, " 'Pusillanimity'?"

"Cowardice," I said.

"My supporters," Callico said, "decent, honest men, both of them, were confronted by General Laird's hired gunman in an attempt to repress the truth."

"Ain't that 'suppress'?" Virgil said.

"I'd use 'suppress,' " I said.

"And you went to the U.S. Military Academy," Virgil said.

"So I must be right," I said.

Virgil nodded.

"But the truth will not be repressed," Callico said. His voice was loud now, and up a pitch. His face was red.

"The commander was a coward at Ralesberg," he shouted, "and a coward at Tyler Creek. His victories were against unarmed women and children who had the misfortune to be in the path of his retreat."

As Callico talked, the general worked his way through the crowd until he stood right in front of Callico. He'd taken off his gloves and held them in his right hand.

"You lie," he said.

His voice sounded like the crack of a bullwhip.

He stepped one step closer and reached up and slapped Callico across the face with the gloves in his right hand. It almost knocked Callico off the chair he stood on. He made a move toward his shoulder holster and stopped himself and got stabilized on the chair.

"Mr. Teagarden is my second," the general said. "I will meet you anywhere. Pistols or sword."

"A duel?" Callico said. "You're challenging me to a fucking duel?"

"I am," the general said.

"A goddamned duel," Virgil murmured to me. "The general's got some sand."

Callico glanced across the room.

"Sergeant Sullivan," he said. "Take this man into custody. Use any requisite force."

Virgil looked at me.

" 'Requisite' means necessary," I said. "Required."

Virgil nodded. Sergeant Sullivan and five policemen assembled in a small squad and pushed through the crowd to General Laird, standing in front of Callico. Chauncey Teagarden moved slightly to the side of the group and looked at General Laird.

"Chauncey takes them on," I said. "We gonna help?"

Virgil stared at the scene silently.

Then he said, "Yes."

I had begun to carry the eight-gauge again as tension had begun to develop in town. I nodded, picked up the eight-gauge from where it leaned against the wall, and moved slowly along the wall to get myself opposite Virgil, so we'd have a nice crossfire if we needed to shoot.

Chauncey saw me move. He nodded his head slightly and looked at General Laird.

"General?" he said.

Laird shook his head.

"Not yet, Chauncey," he said. "It may come to that. But not yet."

I think Callico saw me move, too. He looked at me for a moment and then at Virgil for a moment.

"You are charged with assaulting a police officer," Callico said. "You will be taken to jail and held for hearing."

I saw Chauncey move his shoulders slightly, as if to loosen them.

"My lawyer will bail me out in the morning," the general said. "Not yet, Chauncey."

59

Callico sent one of his many policemen to invite us to come to his office in Reclamation Hall. With its ornate furniture and its dim light, the office had a solemn quality. Callico had lit no lamps, and the rain streaking the big windows filtered what light had made its way through the dark overhead. He sat behind a big desk in the arched bay that looked out over the length of Main Street. At the other end of the long office, two on either side of the door, sat four policemen.

"How many law officers you got now, Amos?" Virgil said.

"We have grown to twenty-five," Callico said. "Including my personal team."

"Palace guard," I said.

Callico shook his head with a smile.

"You don't see the chief of police in Chicago or New York strolling about without escort," Callico said.

Virgil nodded slowly.

"What was it you wanted to see us about?" he said.

"Seen you at the saloon today," Callico said.

"Yep."

"Virgil," Callico said. "Everett. You boys know this town never elected a mayor before."

"Yep."

"I'm not sure it's ready."

Virgil and I said nothing.

"You seen what it was today. I'm trying to tell the truth and my opponent is talking 'bout shooting me."

"Or you him," I said.

"It's barbaric," Callico said. "We cannot have an election when one candidate threatens the life of the other."

"So, what do you do?" I said.

"I may have to cancel the election."

"And who'd run the town?" Virgil said.

"I would," Callico said.

Virgil looked at me and smiled.

"I'll be damned," he said.

"Where'd you get all that information on the general being a coward and a baby killer?" I said.

"Very reliable person," he said.

"That being?" I said.

Callico paused, thinking about it.

"I can't tell you," he said.

"Figured you couldn't," Virgil said. "What was it you wanted from us?"

"Looked to me this morning, when the balloon was sort of getting ready to go up, that you boys was getting ready to side with Laird."

"We was going to side with anybody, be Teagarden," Virgil said. "He helped us out with your Indians."

Callico stared at Virgil.

"For crissake, Virgil," he said. "He's here to kill you."

"I know," Virgil said.

Callico stared at Virgil some more. He didn't get it. I did. We owed Chauncey for the Indians. And he wasn't here to kill Virgil yet. But I'd been with Virgil a long time. Like so many others before him. Callico had never met anybody like Virgil Cole. No one said anything.

"I think this is going to get pretty bad," Callico said finally.

"Sounds like it to me," Virgil said.

"Meanwhile," he said, "I'm prepared to make you boys special deputies reporting only to me. I'll give the same deal to your friend Teagarden."

"Everett?" Virgil said.

236

"Don't want to be a special deputy," I said.

"Me, either," Virgil said. "Can't speak for Chauncey, but it don't seem probable."

"Will you side with Laird?" Callico said.

"Don't know," Virgil said. "You know, Everett?"

"I don't," I said.

"He'll lose," Callico said. "I got twenty-five men. I'll close Appaloosa down and run it like conquered territory until the town is mine and knows it."

"Then what?" Virgil said.

"Then we move on."

"What happens to Appaloosa?"

"Don't know," Callico said. "Won't care. I won't be moving on to something worse."

Callico looked at both of us and shook his head slowly for a while.

"It's sad, really," he said finally. "You boys had a chance to get on board something important here, and you're too dumb to see it."

"Maybe it ain't dumb," Virgil said.

Callico gave a humorless laugh.

"What else could it be."

"Aw, hell, I dunno," Virgil said. "Probably dumb."

He stood. I stood, and we walked down the long office past the palace guard and out the front door.

60

When we came back to Virgil's house in the late afternoon, Chauncey Teagarden was sipping whiskey on the front porch and watching Allie flirt with him.

"Mr. Teagarden has been entertaining me with tales of New Orleans," Allie said when we sat down.

"Entertaining fella," Virgil said, and poured himself a little whiskey.

"He says he knew Mrs. Callico in New Orleans," Allie said.

"The Countess," I said.

"Did you know her, too, Everett?"

"Nope, just what Chauncey has told me."

"Was she really a countess?"

Chauncey glanced at Virgil. Virgil shrugged faintly. And nodded even more faintly.

"Was a whore," Chauncey said.

"A whore?"

"Yes."

"Well," Allie said. "Just because you've been a whore doesn't mean you're always a whore."

"No," Chauncey said.

"People can change. They can grow. And they do," Allie said. "She's turned into a fine lady."

"Surely has," Virgil said. "Also the one that says Laird ran from combat."

"Amelia?" Chauncey said. "How the hell would she know."

"Probably don't," Virgil said.

"You think she made it up?" Chauncey said.

"I do," Virgil said.

"You think Amelia Callico is telling lies about the general?" Allie said.

"Yep."

"Why would she do that?"

"Get her husband elected mayor," Virgil said.

"You and Everett gonna have to take a side here 'fore it's over. Too much shooting gonna be done, and you boys are too good at it not to get pulled in."

"Callico's got twenty-five policemen," I said. "You got how many?"

"Me and Laird's hands," Chauncey said.

"How many gun hands?"

"Me."

"What do you think, Everett?"

"Never liked Callico," I said.

"Hard to like," Virgil said.

"Pony's in Buffalo Springs," I said. "I could ride down and get him."

"That'd be three of you," Chauncey said. "And me makes all we need."

I looked at Virgil. He nodded.

"I'll ride on down and get Pony Flores," I said.

Allie was listening to this as if a new universe was opening up. She poured herself some whiskey and drank it.

"Bring Laurel back, too," she said. "For a visit."

"No," Virgil said. "He'll bring you down there to stay with Laurel. I don't want either of you around town for a time."

"Just like that?" Allie said. "Go gallivanting off with Everett for a two-day trip."

"You can make it in a day," Virgil said. "And keep your hands off Everett."

Allie blushed.

"Virgil," I said. "You spoil everything."

61

I left Allie to stay with Laurel in the little shed next to the livery corral, where she and Pony lived while he wrangled the livery string and broke an occasional mustang.

"She talk?" I said.

"Some," Pony said.

"Enough?" I said.

"Yes."

It was cloudy and gray riding north, but there was no rain.

"She mind you going?" I said.

"When see you, she know why you here," Pony said. "She say she understand."

"Does she?"

"Yes."

"Wish Allie did," I said. "She bitched the whole way down here yesterday."

"Why she bitch?"

I did a high-voiced imitation of Allie.

" 'What if he's killed? What happens to me? This isn't his fight. . . . Why is he involved at all. . . . *If he loved me, he wouldn't . . .' "*

Pony looked at the dark sky.

"Apache man warrior," he said. "Apache woman proud."

"I know," I said.

Pony grinned.

"In land of Blue-Eyed Devil, not so simple," he said. "Man can't always be warrior. Man get to be cowboy and store man and saloon man. And man who sit in office. Not warrior, I just man who saddle horse. Pitch hay. Pick up horse shit. But I go with you and Virgil, I warrior."

"Not everybody wants to be a warrior," I said.

"No. But nobody want to be pick-up-horse-shit man, either," Pony said.

"Some people like it 'cause it's safe, I guess."

"Life not lived to be safe. Safe make you weak," Pony said. "Make you slow. Make you tired."

We pretty much gave the horses their head, keeping them pointed north but letting them pick the trail. Half a day on the trail and it began to rain again. Not too hard but steady. The horses paid no attention. We put on our slickers and buttoned them up and pulled the brims of our hats down and hunched a little forward over the necks of the horses.

"Things turn out the way they heading," I said, "you ain't gonna be tired for a good while."

62

On the following Monday, Callico declared a state of martial law to exist in Appaloosa, and called off the election.

The office of the chief of police is now the highest authority in Appaloosa, the proclamation read. It was signed *Amos A. Callico, chief of police.*

"Ain't martial law supposed to be the Army?" Virgil said.

"Twenty-five policemen in a town this size is an Army," I said.

"That's a fact," Virgil said.

The rain that had been coming down steadily for more than a week was tapering, and as we sat drinking coffee in Café Paris, it had stopped completely.

"Question is," I said, "what's the general going to do?"

"Yep."

"Which," I said, "will then lead to the question what are we going to do?"

"You didn't go down and get Pony," Virgil said. " 'Cause we needed a fourth for whist."

I nodded.

Chauncey Teagarden came in with his slicker unbuttoned. He hung his white hat on the rack and sat down at our table.

"Ain't raining," he said.

"Will again," I said.

"Often does," Chauncey said. "The general would like you boys to come out and see him, soon's you can."

"The election?" I said.

"You boys heard about that," Chauncey said.

"We did," I said.

"General says he can't do that," Chauncey said.

"He can do what people will let him do," Virgil said.

"Think that's what he might want to talk about," Chauncey said.

"In fact," Virgil said, "might just as well ride back on out there with you when you go."

"That'll be soon's I finish my coffee," Chauncey said.

"Okay," Virgil said. "Everett, bring the eight-gauge. Looks impressive."

63

The rain had picked up again by the time we got to the Lazy L. We hung our coats and hats in the front hall and went into the living room to sit by the big stone fireplace and let the fire dry us out.

The houseboy poured whiskey.

"Fine-looking decanter," Virgil said.

He loved learning a new word and tried to use it as often as possible. The results weren't always pretty, but he got this one right.

"I'm going after Callico," the general said.

"So I understand," Virgil said.

"I employ cattle hands. Not gunmen. They were ready to fight the Indian raid, self-defense. They are not ready to fight Callico and his police force."

"No volunteers," Virgil said.

The general drank some whiskey.

"None," he said.

"Bad odds," Virgil said.

The general nodded.

"They're cowboys," he said. "That's what they signed on for."

"And what did you sign on for?" I said.

"You remember what they taught us at West Point about honor and duty and country."

I smiled.

"Vaguely," I said.

"I fought on the wrong side in the wrong war because I felt to do otherwise would have been dishonorable. I still think so."

"That war's over," I said.

"I cannot let this bandit take over the town like some Mongolian warlord," the general said.

"Not sure Appaloosa's worth dying for," I said.

"We'll help you," Virgil said.

"I will pay you well," the general said. "And any men you can enlist."

"This one's free," Virgil said.

"Our history will be put aside for the duration," the general said.

I was looking at Virgil. He generally had the moral scruples of a tarantula. And he declined to work for free.

"You work for free, you're just a gunman," he always said. *"You do it 'cause you like it."*

Which was maybe some kind of moral scruple.

"Chauncey," Virgil said. "You're in."

"Surely am," Chauncey said.

"Pony?"

"*Sí.*"

"Everett and me, that's four."

"I am five," the general said.

Virgil almost spoke but held it back.

"You think Cato and Rose might come down from Resolution for this?"

"I'd say they owe us," I said.

"That'd make seven," Virgil said. "Anybody got anybody else?"

No one spoke.

"Okay, twenty-five to seven," Virgil said. "And since the seven is us, odds ain't bad."

He held his glass out.

"Reach me that there decanter, Pony," he said.

Pony looked at him blankly.

"That there fancy bottle," Virgil said. "Called a decanter."

Pony nodded and poured Virgil a drink. Everyone else had a second.

"You have, I assume, engaged in this kind of operation before," the general said.

"Yes, sir," Virgil said.

"Do you wish my help in the planning?"

"No, sir," Virgil said.

"I rather thought you wouldn't," the general said. "What's the first step?"

"Pony'll ride up and get Cato and Rose," Virgil said.

"Do you have a plan?" the general said.

"Need to get an idea of Callico's plan, and adjust to it," Virgil said.

"A strategy, then?"

"Kill Callico and not get killed doin' it," Virgil said. "But first we gotta let him know we're coming and see what preparations he makes."

"How you going to do that?" the general said.

Virgil looked at me. I grinned.

"We'll tell Allie," I said.

64

When Pony came back from Resolution
with Cato and Rose, he brought them
straight to the house. Virgil introduced Allie. She curtsied and went for the jug of
corn whiskey.

"Pony tell you anything on the ride
down?" Virgil said.

Rose laughed.

"Riding down here with Pony and Cato
can be lonely business," he said.

"Okay," Virgil said. "What you see drinking whiskey at the table is what we go to
war with."

Cato and Rose both looked at Chauncey.

Rose said, "Frank Rose. This here's Cato
Tillson."

"Chauncey Teagarden," he said.

"Like your shirt," Rose said.

Chauncey nodded.

"Like yours, too," he said.

"Besides the six of us," Virgil said, "there's

a general got to be in on it."

"A general?" Rose said.

"From the Confederate states army."

"Long-in-the-tooth general," Rose said.

"Yes."

"He think he's in charge?"

"No," Virgil said.

"He think you're in charge?" Rose said.

"Yep."

"No disrespect, Everett," Rose said. "But Virgil ain't in charge, me and Cato go back to Resolution."

"I'm in charge," Virgil said.

"Got a plan yet?" Cato said.

"We're developing one," Virgil said. "Tell 'em, Everett, if you would. You being a West Point graduate."

"Allie here is a close friend of Callico's wife, Amelia, the Countess of Storyville."

"Storyville," Rose said.

"Yep. But Allie don't care — they are pals. So she lets it slide that we're coming after Callico and tells her to warn Callico but not tell who we are."

"And she thinks the Countess will do that?"

"No," I said. "Allie's playing dumb. We know Mrs. Callico will give us away."

"But then," Virgil said. "He got two choices: comes right after us or, two, he sets

251

up for us to come after him."

"Either way we're setting ourselves up," Rose said.

" 'Cept they don't know we know they know," Virgil said. "So we watch them watching us."

"You think they'll come for us?" Cato said.

"No," Virgil said. "Man wants to be president. Looks better if he defeats a bunch of ruffians who attacked him."

"How 'bout the wife?" Rose said.

"Lady Macbeth," Chauncey said.

"Who?" Rose said.

"Bad woman in a play," I said. "She wants him to be president, too."

"How good are his constables?" Cato said.

"Don't know yet," I said. "Pretty sure not as good as us."

"But pretty sure twenty-five to six," Rose said.

"Seven," Virgil said.

"The general," Rose said.

"Yeah."

"Twenty-five to six, and a geezer," Rose said.

"He'll carry his weight," Virgil said.

"He better," Frank said.

"He will," Chauncey said.

65

It was late. Chauncey went back to the Lazy L. Cato and Rose went to sleep in Virgil's shed. Allie was cleaning up, and Virgil and I sat on the porch and looked at the first clear sky we'd seen in two weeks. There were stars.

"Allie," I said.

"Odd," Virgil said. "Ain't it."

"She worships Amelia Callico," I said. "She thinks Amelia Callico is the Queen of New Orleans."

"She gets faint if the Countess looks at her," Virgil said.

"And she don't want this fight to happen," I said.

"She don't," Virgil said.

"But she sets the trap on her 'cause you asked her to."

"Allie loves me," Virgil said.

"Except when she doesn't," I said.

Virgil sipped his whiskey.

"She always loves me," he said. "Some-times other stuff gets in the way."

"She wants to be more than she is," I said. "She cheats on you. She gets so sucked up into her self that she can't see you for a while. She gets lost. You go find her. She strays off. You bring her back. You love her."

"I do," Virgil said.

"Why?"

"Don't know," Virgil said.

We poured ourselves more whiskey.

"But you do," I said.

"Yep."

"You ever spend time thinking about it?"

"Nope."

I grinned.

"No," I said. "You wouldn't."

"I like it," Virgil said. "It works for me. Why fuck around with it."

"Don't spend much time figuring yourself out, either," I said.

"Same thing," Virgil said.

"You like yourself," I said.

Virgil grinned.

"So, why fuck with it?" he said.

"You know why you're getting into General Laird's fight?" I said.

"Killed his kid," Virgil said.

"Feel guilty 'bout that?"

"Nope," Virgil said. "Kid gave me no

choice. Don't mean I can't help his old man out."

"And we don't like Callico, do we?" I said.

"No," Virgil said. "We don't."

"And we do kind of like putting together a little firefight like this."

Virgil drank some corn whiskey and held it in his mouth and looked up at the stars. He nodded slowly.

"We do," he said.

66

"New moon," General Laird said.

Six of us sat our horses back from the ridgeline in the near-perfect darkness above Appaloosa.

"Yep," Virgil said.

"Knew that when you planned this," the general said.

"Did," Virgil said.

Almost noiselessly, Pony Flores guided his horses up from the right slope and in beside Virgil.

"How's he do that?" Chauncey said to me. "I know he's quiet, but how's he make the horse quiet?"

Pony heard him.

"Chiricahua," he murmured to Chauncey.

"Or Mex," Chauncey said.

"Or both," Pony said.

"How is it down there?" Virgil said.

He never got nervous, but he did focus sometimes, and this was one of those times.

"Done what you say he do, Jefe," Pony said.

"Set up an ambush," Virgil said.

"Sí."

Downslope a ways five extra horses were tethered. They would blow softly now and then in the darkness.

"Where's he got 'em?" Virgil said.

"I show," Pony said.

We moved down slope a little and dismounted. I got a lantern going, and we crouched together, watching, while Pony scratched out a sort of map in the dirt.

"Have two on second floor, Boston House," Pony said, and marked it.

"One on roof of Golden Palace." He drew an X.

"Three in livery corral. Behind wagon." He drew three X's.

When Pony was finished Virgil counted the X's.

"I get fifteen," he said.

"Five alone," I said.

"We can take them out?" Virgil said to Pony. "Quiet?"

"Sí," Pony said. "The ones alone. Maybe two on roof at jail."

"You think you can take out two men in the dark without making any noise."

"Chiricahua," Pony said. "Kill many men

257

on roof."

"Chiricahua better not fuck this up," Virgil said. "Blow the whole goddamned project if there's noise."

"*Sí.*"

"On the jail roof," I said.

"*Sí.*"

"I won't tell you how to do your work," Virgil said.

"We pull it off, he'll have a lot fewer men than he thinks he's got," I said.

"Where's the rest?" Virgil said.

"Jail," Pony said.

"Right below Pony," I said.

"With Callico?" Virgil said.

"*Sí.*"

Virgil studied the sketch in the dirt for a bit. Then he stood and remounted and rode to a spot just below the ridgeline. It was too dark to be seen, but Virgil was always careful. He sat and looked down at Appaloosa for a while.

"We get the first part cleaned up and settle in," Virgil said. "Then just before dawn the horses go in."

"Somebody gotta drive them," I said.

"I'll do that," General Laird said.

"Good chance you don't survive," Virgil said.

"No need," the general said. "I'm seventy-seven years old. My son is dead. I'm the one you can spare for this. No need to survive."

Nobody said anything.

"I'll stick here with him," Teagarden said.

"Okay," Virgil said. "Just before dawn. We pull this off and we're all in place. You bring the horses in, bunched up together so they can't really tell if there are riders. When they start shooting, you get down in the saddle and get the hell out of there."

"Okay," he said. "We may as well start. Who wants the Golden Palace?"

"I know the place," Cato said. "I'll take it."

"Before you begin," Laird said.

We waited.

"I am seventy-seven," Laird said again. "All I have left in the world is my ranch. I was going to leave it to my son. But Virgil Cole killed my son. Because I was a powerful man, I told my son he was a powerful man. I was a soldier all my life. Power, I told him, comes from the muzzle of a gun. He took it to heart. Because I was powerful, my son thought he was powerful. Because I was powerful, people treated my son as if he were powerful. I thought he was. He thought he was. And it got him killed by Virgil Cole."

Nobody spoke in the darkness. The horses stood quiet, waiting, the way they did.

"That is my fault," Laird said. "Virgil Cole did what he had to do."

We were still.

"Chauncey, I don't want you to kill him," Laird said.

"Hell, General, Callico probably gonna kill us both, anyway," Chauncey said.

"I want you men to witness this," Laird said. "My only connection to my son is through the man who killed him. And he's a good man. If I die here, or when I die somewhere, I want Cole to have the ranch."

"Virgil?" I said.

"Yes."

"You understand what you're doing?"

"Yes," Laird said.

There was a moment more of silence.

Then Laird said, "And so does Virgil Cole."

In the darkness, Virgil said, "I do."

"We're all witness," I said.

"Then let's get to it," Virgil said. We all dismounted, took our spurs off, and began down the hill toward town. Being silent in the dark made it slow going.

My man was behind the Chinese laundry, barricaded behind some big wash cauldrons, with, in daylight, a clear line of sight at the open space in front of the jail.

I remembered moving in on a Comanche camp through a dark Texas night. The horses held by squad back from the scene, the troopers spread out on each side of me, the silence so pressing that you didn't want to breathe. Except this time I was alone. I stashed the eight-gauge on the far wall of the laundry. It would be in my way for what I had to do now. But it would be very handy later.

I took the bowie knife from its scabbard. I don't enjoy knives much, but there didn't seem any other way. I went very slowly, feeling my way with the toe of my boot through the littered laundry lot. It took so long that I was afraid dawn would arrive before I got to him.

But it didn't.

And I cut his throat soundlessly before he ever knew he was dead, and took his place behind the wash pots.

67

So far no noise. The silence was as thick as the darkness. I edged my way back to the side wall of the laundry and retrieved my eight-gauge. Then I inched back to my spot next to the dead man behind the laundry kettles. Somewhere off to my right, out a ways on the incipient prairie, some sort of night animal snuffled for a moment. Then, again, nothing. To my left, I knew, in Chester Hamlin's Dry Goods were two of Callico's riflemen. Across the street were two more on the roof of Rockenwagner's Hardware.

I listened to my own breath going in and out softly. In the east the sky was less black. I heard the horses. In the first dim light of morning they came, bunched up tight together, little more than a dark, moving mass as they came up Main Street toward the jail. And paused. A shot exploded from the jailhouse, and one of the horses reared and screamed and went down. I waited, watching the muzzle flashes as Callico's men opened up from their rooftops and storefronts. The jail doors opened, and the rest of Callico's men poured into the street, shooting into the cluster of surging horses fanning out around them.

I felt bad about the horses.

From the roof of the jail, Pony Flores started shooting down into the crowd of policemen in the street below him. The rest of us, from our own storefronts and rooftops, began firing. Callico's people were confused, then panicked. They didn't know who was shooting or where it was coming from. On the roof of the dry goods store the two shooters stood up, looking to see what was happening. I picked one off with each barrel of the eight-gauge. It's easy to hit things with an eight-gauge shotgun.

In front of me, the street was littered with struggling horses and fallen men. Thick smoke drifted over them. From somewhere, one of us picked off the two men on Rockenwagner's roof. The sound of gunfire was steady. Some of the horses screamed. Some of the men screamed.

And then it stopped. The chaos was too much for Callico's men. They broke and ran, and in barely a minute, the street in front of the jail was empty of fighting. It wasn't silent. Too many men and animals were hurt. But there was no gunfire, and it seemed almost still because of it.

It was daylight.

Virgil Cole walked out of the alley near the bank, and in his almost stately way walked down to the jail. In the middle of the wounded horses and men, he paused and squatted down. With the eight-gauge loaded, I walked out and joined him. He was sitting on his heels beside Chauncey Teagarden, who was sprawled protectively over the body of General Laird, with both Colts still in his hand.

"Couldn't get him down in time," Chauncey said, and sat up, and rolled back on his heels and stood. "Not sure he wanted to."

He put both of his fancy handguns back into their holsters.

"You did what you could," Virgil said.

Chauncey nodded.

"I did," he said.

Pony came down from the jail's roof and stood with us. Cato and Rose appeared. There was a thin line of blood on Rose's cheek, as if a bullet had kicked up a splinter.

He looked around at the street.

"Damn," he said. "We're good."

Virgil walked to the open door of the jail.

"Callico," he said.

From inside Amos Callico said, "I'm not shooting with you, Cole."

"Come out here," Virgil said.

"I'm not shooting," Callico said. "My hands are empty."

He came through the door with a gun in his hand and got off one shot at Virgil before Virgil killed him.

Callico had a clean shot from a short distance, and he missed. I have always thought it was because he was shooting at the great Virgil Cole.

"Blue-Eyed Devil," Pony said, "not speak from heart."

"Sometimes they don't," Virgil said.

68

Virgil and I sat alone on his porch in the thick darkness, drinking corn whiskey.

"Think the general wanted to die?" I said.

"Don't think he cared," Virgil said.

"Whatcha gonna do with that ranch?" I said.

"Give it to Pony and Laurel," Virgil said.

"The whole fucking ranch?" I said.

"I ain't no rancher," Virgil said.

"And you think Pony is?"

"Chance to find out," Virgil said.

"What if you give it to him and he loses it?" I said.

"Be his to lose," Virgil said.

"Laurel might help him keep it," I said.

"Might," Virgil said.

There was a lamp lit inside the house, and it was enough for us to see each other. Virgil drank some corn whiskey.

"Pony's going down to Buffalo Springs tomorrow to get her," I said.

"Allie, too," Virgil said.

"Think Allie'll want the ranch?" I said.

"Sure," Virgil said.

"But she won't get it."

"No," Virgil said.

I poured a little whiskey from the jug. Above us there was still no moon, but the clouds had moved away and there were stars. I looked at them for a while.

"Couldn't be with Allie," I said, "could you? If you paid too much attention to what she wanted."

"Allie wants everything," Virgil said.

"Be jumping around like a grasshopper," I said. "In July."

"Would," Virgil said.

"She'll get over it," I said.

"She will," Virgil said.

Virgil sipped some more whiskey. I liked whiskey. I didn't like how it tasted. But I liked the way it made me feel, unless I drank too much. Virgil, on the other hand, never seemed to feel different when he drank whiskey. It was as if he just liked the taste.

We didn't want to sleep. A big gunfight is exhausting. Even if it's short. And we were exhausted. But we didn't want to let it all go yet. So we sat in the starry darkness with each other and the whiskey.

"Wonder if that stallion's still up in the

hills with his mares," Virgil said.

"The Appaloosa?"

"Yeah."

"Suppose he is," I said.

"Strutting around stiff-legged with his tail up and his ears back."

"If you come near the mares," I said.

"Think he loves them mares?" Virgil said.

"They're his," I said.

"Likes to fuck 'em," Virgil said.

"Sure," I said.

"Think that's all of it?" Virgil said.

I shrugged.

"They're his," I said.

Virgil nodded silently. He poured some whiskey, took a sip, then held the glass up and looked through the clear whiskey for a time at the lamplight from the parlor.

"So," I said. "We ain't gonna be ranchers."

"Nope."

"Don't see no future to the barroom protection service," I said. "Now that Callico's gone."

"Nope."

"So, what do we do now?" I said.

"Figure the town might need couple of experienced lawmen," Virgil said.

"Since we shot up the previous," I said.

"Yep."

"And we know how to do that," I said.

"We do," Virgil said.

"So, we sit tight," I said. "See what develops."

"Be my plan," Virgil said.

He stood and carried his whiskey to the far corner of the porch and looked into the darkness.

"Remember the general talking 'bout power coming from the end of a gun?" Virgil said.

"Yep. Taught his kid that. I guess he wished he hadn't," I said.

Virgil was silent. Far out on the prairie, a coyote barked. Then silence.

"Thing is," Virgil said. "He was right."

"Depends on who's holding the gun, don't it?" I said.

"S'pose is does," Virgil said.